Salem Unleashed

John Watson

INTERNATIONAL BESTSELLING AUTHOR

JOHN WATSON

Now operating under the codename Salem, Rebecca Grainger is part of a crack squad of secret operatives funded by eccentric billionaire Spencer Thorn.

There are still creatures on the loose, including Rebecca's mother Raven, a powerful witch who will stop at nothing to rule the world. The team needs to track them down before Raven can deliver Hell on earth.

With her previously hidden powers now unleashed, Salem is ready to go on the hunt in the ultimate battle of good versus evil.

Dedication

For every reader of my previous books.

You all help make the next one possible.

Chapter One

Rebecca lay on the cot, tossing and turning as sleep refused to come. Confident in her powers, she had no concerns about the upcoming raid on Alcatraz. Instead, it was what would come after that gnawed at her. Would Terry look at her the same way, and would she have a relationship with the only people she had known as her parents?

In her mind, it felt as though Rebecca was dead and that Salem was how she now identified herself. With her powers turned on, the idea of flicking them off again seemed unappealing.

Rolling over, she focused on the door and began controlling the lock with her mind, marveling at how easy it was to slide it open and closed. While she fiddled with the lock, Salem raised her arm and willed a glass of water on the table across the room into her hand. All of it felt strange, but also somehow natural, like these were acts she should be performing.

Sitting up, she took a sip of water and closed her eyes, concentrating on the sounds outside her spartan room.

Just behind her walls, she heard rodents and insects scuttling around in search of food scraps. The guards outside her door talked in hushed tones, the occasional word becoming clear. If she really focused, Salem knew that she would hear the entire conversation, but she cast her mind further, searching for Terry and hoping that he was somewhere nearby.

Her search came back empty, and she could feel the anger begin to brew inside. Exhaling slowly, Salem fought to regain her inner calm, not wishing to expend too much energy before making the trip to Alcatraz and potentially coming face to face with her mother.

The sound of footsteps coming down the hallway beyond her room snapped her back to the present. With a wave of her hand, she unlocked the door and opened it, smiling when she saw Drake, hand raised and ready to knock. "Come in," Salem said, sending the glass of water back to the table.

If Drake was surprised by the glass floating across the room, he didn't show it. He gave it the merest glance as he strode into the room, followed by Bits and Bytes.

"To what do I owe the pleasure?" Salem asked, doing nothing to hide the sarcasm in her voice.

Pulling a cheap plastic chair over beside her bed, Drake sat and studied her for a moment before speaking. "Mr. Thorn would like to know if you are comfortable."

Glancing around the room, Salem smirked. "It's not the Hilton, but it'll do."

Drake nodded. "He also asked me to pass on some news."

Salem pushed herself up and leaned forward, the springs on the mattress groaning in protest as she moved. "Okay."

"It's about your mom and dad."

"Selina and Craig, you mean? I think we are all past that pretense now."

"Sure, Selina and Craig."

Salem felt her skin warm as she wormed her way inside Lionel Drake's head, looking for the truth behind the lies she was almost certainly about to hear. As hard as she pushed, there was nothing to see. It was akin to trying to read a wet book whose ink had bled, making the words illegible.

Drake's left eye twitched slightly as he spoke. "I'm afraid there was an accident, and…"

"What kind of accident?" Salem continued to probe.

"A vehicle collision. Craig died on the scene. We did all we could for your mo… for Selina, but she also passed. I'm sorry."

She looked beyond Drake to Bits and Bytes, who stood by the door, heads down, refusing to make eye contact. Salem probed the IT team but ran across the same issue. "What about Terry?"

"What about him?" Drake asked.

"Where is he?"

Your boyfriend is safe. I have another member of our security team staying with him at a safe house. No harm will come his way, I assure you."

Salem leaned forward until she was almost nose to nose with Drake. "He had better be safe. If anything happens to him, I will hold you responsible. Are we clear?"

The chair scraped loudly across the concrete floor as Drake pushed it backwards and stood. "He'll be fine. I'll be back to brief you before we move on Alcatraz."

"When are we leaving."

Pausing at the door, his back to Salem, Drake said, "Soon. Get some rest. I have a feeling you might need it."

***

Once they were clear of the building adjacent to the Thorn Industries main warehouse, Drake smiled at Bits and Bytes. "Did you feel it?"

Bits shuddered. "She was definitely inside my head. Not an experience I'd care to repeat anytime soon."

"Like ants crawling under the skin," Bytes added.

Fishing in his left ear, Drake plucked out a small metallic disc that looked like a watch battery. "I think we can agree that your little blocking device worked like a charm."

"What makes you so confident?" Bytes asked.

Drake thought about the pile of destroyed mannequins and targets back in the space where Salem trained. "Because, boys, I am still alive."

Chapter Two

Waves of fatigue washed over Raven, making it close to impossible to lift her head off the pillow. The Rake knelt by the bed and pawed at her, telling her that it was time to move. She felt his despair and knew it was time to move.

Forcing herself up, she followed the creature out of the prison and down the path to the dock, where she saw the Nuckelavee laying on its side, front hooves pawing at the ground.

Raven forced herself to move, her legs muscles burning as she picked up the pace. "I'm coming."

When she reached the beast, the rider was in the process of pulling himself free of the horse whose flesh he shared. He tore free with a snapping of tendons, grunting with the effort.

Raven reached out and placed a hand on his shoulder, her other hand resting on the exposed flank of the horse, which was rising and falling slowly with each shallow breath.

"Leave us be, lass. We are dying," the rider said in his thick Scottish brogue.

"Be still. Let me work."

Placing a bony hand on Raven's arm, the rider pulled her hand away from his mount. "It'll not work." He nodded towards the bay. "There is freshwater out there. It's like poison flowing through our veins."

"Damn you. Let me try."

The rider pulled himself across the ground and lay across the body of the horse. "Save your strength, lass. You have done enough. We will die free. Better that than wastin' away in some damnable prison."

Raven moved back and watched as the rider whispered in the ear of his horse, his hand caressing her flank. They both stopped moving at the same time, their hearts stopping in unison.

She stood and raised her face to the sky, letting loose a scream that sent tremors through the concrete beneath her feet.

The Rake backed away in fear, head bowed in supplication.

Raven turned to face the creature, her eyes blazing with fury. "Bring the others to me, right now."

She watched as the Rake sped away on all fours. When he disappeared from sight, she closed her eyes and reached out with her mind, hoping to connect with her daughter.

Where are you, child?

***

Salem awoke with a gasp, clutching at the bedsheets, which were damp with sweat. She looked around the dimly lit room, looking for the source of the voice that had pulled her out of a fitful sleep.

Lifting herself out of bed, she stepped into the small bathroom attached to her sleeping quarters and flicked on the overhead light. The single fluorescent light flickered as it came to life, filling the space with an incessant hum that sounded like a mosquito buzzing by her ear.

Salem rubbed her eyes and turned on the sink faucet with her mind. The cold water felt good as she splashed it on her face before cupping her hands and gulping down a mouthful.

"Where are you, child?"

With a start, Salem stepped away from the sink and stared into the mirror that sat above it, expecting to see someone standing behind her. There was no one there.

Flicking off the light, Salem sat on the toilet seat and closed her eyes, embracing the dark. "I am here."

"I hear you. Are you safe?"

Salem tapped the heel of her hand against the side of her head, trying to pull herself free from the final stages of sleep.

"Rebecca?"

"Mother?"

"Yes. Are you safe?"

"I'm not sure. These people are not to be trusted, but I think they fear me."

Salem jumped at the sound of thumping on her door. "Is everything alright in there?"

"What?"

The guard rattled the door handle, looking to get inside. "I hear voices," he said, as he struggled with the lock that Salem was keeping in place.

"I'm fine. I had a nightmare."

The rattling stopped, and things went still again.

"If they are with Thorn, they are not your friends."

"I…"

"I can hear your thoughts, child. Speak to me in your mind."

Moving back to her bed, Salem laid down and placed her arm over her eyes. *"Can you still hear me?"*

"I can, and I can feel your fear. I am coming for you. I just need a moment a day or two to rest. They will not know what hit them."

Salem sat up straight, heart thudding in her chest. *"They are coming for you. They know where you are."*

There was a moment of silence that seemed suddenly deafening.

"Mother."

"When?"

"Soon."

"Rebecca, you cannot come with them."

"I don't have a choice. They have my boyfriend. I need to play along until I know he is safe."

Silence again.

"I'll be ready."

Salem felt pressure at her temples for a split second as the connection to her mother closed. She rose and moved to the door, throwing it open, and stepping out into the corridor. The guards dropped to their knees weapons pointed in her direction.

"Put those away." Salem nonchalantly flicked her hand, sending the guns skittering down the hallway. "Tell your boss I need to have a chat."

***

Spencer Thorn sat in his electric wheelchair and stared out his office window, seeing nothing but a swirling mass of dense fog. "It's bad enough she got out, but now that bitch has ruined my view," he muttered.

"What was that, sir?" Drake asked.

Wheeling around to face Drake, Thorn waved a dismissive hand. "Nothing. Tell me more about the blocking device our little geniuses developed."

Drake placed a plastic box that looked like a wireless earbud charger on the desk and pushed it across to the billionaire. "It's in there."

Thorn opened the case and lifted out the circular device, holding it up for closer inspection. "So, you're telling me that you tried this and that it works?"

Drake nodded. "I told her that Selina and Craig were dead. We all felt her fishing around in our heads, but she got nothing."

"Magnificent. I'm assuming there are enough for all of us making the trip?"

The idea of telling his boss that this was not a babysitting mission crossed his mind, but instead, Drake played the dutiful soldier. "Of course, sir."

A knock on the office door interrupted the conversation.

"Enter," Thorn called out.

One of the guards chosen to look after Salem stepped into the office, his eyes darting around nervously.

Drake rose from his seat and yelled at the guard, "Why are you away from your post? And where the hell is your weapon."

"Sh-she removed it, sir."

"Explain yourself," Drake demanded.

"The witch. She took away our weapons without laying a hand on us."

"Where is she now?" Drake asked, unholstering his sidearm.

"In her room. She is demanding to speak to Mr. Thorn."

The billionaire wheeled himself out from behind his desk and pulled up beside Drake. He placed the metallic device in his ear and said, "Looks like I'm going to get to test this thing myself."

Chapter Three

Salem stood in the middle of her room, arms folded across her chest, and waited for Thorn to maneuver his powerchair into the tight space. She laughed aloud when he bumped against the table and toppled the glass sitting on top.

"Clumsy me," Thorn said with a smile, his anger simmering just below the surface.

"Accidents happen. I mean, look at your face," Salem jabbed.

The part of Thorn's face that was visible flushed red, the color bleeding down to his neck and threatening to stain his pristine white shirt collar. "Someone is feeling a tad feisty today. I'm told you wanted to see me, Miss Grainger."

"Rebecca Grainger is dead, at least for the moment. My name is Salem."

Thorn waved away the comment as he regained his composure. "Whatever you say, dear. None of it matters to me." He flicked away a piece of lint from his suit jacket and turned his attention back to Salem. "What do you want?"

"A couple of things. First, I want to talk to my boyfriend, plus I want to know the details of our proposed trip to The Rock."

"The first isn't possible," Drake said. "He is in a safe house that has no means of communication in or out."

"Don't feed me bullshit, Lionel," Salem scoffed. "How do you keep in contact with your team out there?"

"I don't need to. There is only one road in and out. Trust me, they won't be bothered."

Salem stared down the mercenary, thinking about the ways she would like to hurt him. As she did that, she reached out and slipped inside the mind of Spencer Thorn, only to be met with the same brick wall as earlier.

"We can, though, supply some details on our mission," Thorn said, a milky tear dripping from his ruined left eyeball and onto the silver mask covering that side of his face.

She probed deeper and took some delight in seeing tears begin to flow freely from his eye.

Thorn squirmed in his chair but still managed a smile that looked more like a grimace. "Would you care to hear those details, or are we done here?"

Beginning to feel the strain of using her powers to no avail, Salem pulled out of Thorn's mind and relaxed. "Let's hear it."

"Lionel, if you would care to take the floor."

Noticing the white fluid running down his boss's mask, Drake pulled a handkerchief from the pocket of his dress shirt and handed it to Thorn before beginning to speak. "We shall depart from this facility by helicopter at six a.m. sharp. I expect you to be ready fifteen minutes prior to our departure."

"I should warn you that I'm not much of a morning person."

Ignoring the remark, Drake continued. "There will be two birds. You will occupy one with

Bits and Bytes, as well as two security personnel. Myself, Mr. Thorn, and two more of my team will take the other."

"That's a lot of men," Salem said. "A lot of potential for trigger fingers."

Thorn wheeled forward a touch and cleared his throat. "I believe I already mentioned, Miss Grainger, that this is a retrieval mission, not some mass execution."

"And I believe I told you that my name is Salem."

Drake stepped between the two, hands raised in an effort to calm the impending blowout. "Can we please focus on the task at hand?"

"My apologies to you both. Please, continue," Thorn said.

"As just mentioned, we are looking to recapture the escaped creatures, so I would ask, Salem, that you try to show some restraint."

Gritting her teeth and holding back her anger, Salem nodded.

"We will have limited space in the choppers, which means that we may need to sacrifice one of the escapees," Thorn continued.

Unable to restrain herself further, Salem spoke loudly. "I hope you're not talking about my mother. Losing a trio of parental types in the space of twenty-four hours might be more than I can take. You've both seen how I get when I'm upset."

Spinning his powerchair around, Thorn headed for the door. "This conversation is over." He looked down at his wristwatch. A little more than two hours before we leave. Please try to be ready and on your best behavior, Salem."

She watched him go and then turned her attention back to Drake. "Not my mother, right?"

"No. The Wenlutah. We have a replacement coming in a couple of days." Drake gave a little nod and followed his boss out the door, which narrowly avoided contact with as Salem threw it closed.

She was tired, but Salem knew that sleep would not come. Hopping onto her bed, she hoisted herself up and peered out a narrow window sitting just below the ceiling. She didn't think that any pilot worth his salt would fly in such conditions, but she decided to try and warn her mother, just in case they did make it out.

***

The water lapped against the dock, the rhythmic splashing bringing a sense of exterior calm to Raven that she didn't feel inside.

The chance to escape Thorn's prison was one that she knew she had to take, but if she were honest with herself, she didn't know what to do now. Two of the creatures that had escaped with her were now dead, and Raven knew that she had to accept some blame in that.

What was the end goal? Was it to slip back into a life like she's lived before being caught? She didn't believe that possible, for as powerful and smart as she was, she could not compete with Thorn and his money. Raven knew that he would spend whatever it took to get his exhibits back. What he might do to her once she was back in his grasp was not worth thinking about.

"Mother?"

Raven had hoped to hear from her daughter again, but the voice in her head was still a surprise.

"My child. How are you?"

"Scared. They are coming, and..."

"And taking you with them," Raven finished. *"When?"*

"In less than two hours. Time for you to move, but if you do, leave the Wenlutah behind. That is how they know where you are."

"No. I am responsible for them. Let these men come. We will be ready."

"I will do what I can to help, Mother."

Raven had felt dead inside for as long as she could remember, but it now felt as though blood was reaching her heart again, making it beat, making her care. *"I will do all I can to protect you, child. Are they coming by water?"*

"By air. Helicopters, but I don't think they can fly in this fog."

"I will clear a path for them."

"Why would you do that?"

"This has to end, Salem. I will either be free or die fighting to be so. I will see you soon."

Raven closed off her mind, feeling her daughter reach out and try to continue the conversation. There was nothing more to say. It was time to ready the troops and prepare for the arrival of the enemy.

Looking out beyond The Rock, Raven could barely make out the lights blinking atop the Golden Gate Bridge. The sky above was nothing more than a swirling mass of grey fog. Placing her hands on her abdomen, she closed her eyes and began to gently blow.

The fog twisted and turned upon itself, and ever so slowly began to break apart.

Chapter Four

Salem sat on the edge of the bed and waited for Drake to arrive. The guards were no longer posted outside, her display of power against them seen as a sign that their presence was no longer required.

Before they left, she had probed inside their minds, surprised that access was so easy. She found nothing there to help her, though. The men had been nothing more than mindless minions, the lowest of the low on the Thorn totem pole. She wasn't sure if she should be offended at that fact, but the more Salem considered it, the more it seemed that their lack of any knowledge of the ins and outs of Thorns business dealings was probably why they had been chosen.

Hearing a door open at the end of the hallway, Salem rose and tried to get her mind right. This mission was all about making sure that Terry remained safe and that her mother remained free. How to make both of those things happen was the

29

issue. Salem was sure that Thorn would not look kindly on her playing any role in maintaining Raven's freedom.

Drake rapped on the door and stepped inside, looking like a man ready to do battle. The five o'clock shadow and designer clothing were gone in favor of combat attire and a clean-shaven look that showed off a powerful square jaw.

"Good morning, Lionel," Salem said with a smile.

He seemed surprised by the pleasantries, probably expecting a mouthful of vitriol, but he returned the smile and said, "Good morning to you. Are you ready to go?"

"I'm not sure. Do I need to bring anything?"

Drake pulled a pack off his shoulder and handed it to Salem. "There's a clean set of clothing in there that might be more suitable than what you are wearing now."

Salem looked down at her torn T-shirt, soiled sweatpants, and cheap sneakers, feeling inclined to agree. "I suppose you're right. We aren't going to Wal-Mart after all."

"I'll wait outside while you change. Do it quickly, please."

Tossing her dirty clothes aside, Salem slipped on the fatigues that Drake had delivered. She tied back her red locks with a hair band and surveyed herself in the mirror. Camo was not what she would have ordinarily chosen as a fashion statement, but it was certainly better than what she'd previously had on.

Salem stepped into the hallway, closing and locking the room door with a flick of the wrist.

Drake scowled and shook his head. "You may want to preserve some of that for our trip."

"I've got plenty in reserve," Salem said, jogging down the hallway. "I'm not worried. Maybe you should be."

Remaining stone-faced, Drake wheeled around and set off at a brisk pace. "Choppers leave in fifteen. Let's go."

They headed out of the building and into a waiting Jeep, which took off before they had time to get their seatbelts fastened.

Salem fiddled with the seatbelt, but she struggled to get it engaged as the Jeep bounded over uneven terrain, the driver seemingly oblivious to the thick fog surrounding them.

"Can he even see where he's going?" Salem asked, gripping tightly to the side of the open-topped vehicle.

"Night vision goggles, with some modifications from Bits and Bytes," Drake replied.

"I hope our pilots have those, too. I don't see us going anywhere in this weather."

The rise lasted no more than a couple of minutes, but it felt like forever. Stepping out of the Jeep, Salem rubbed her tailbone, which felt bruised and battered beyond belief.

It looked as though they were standing in the middle of nowhere, but as Drake led them through the fog, shapes began to emerge in the near distance.

It was still tough to see, but Salem could make out a pair of helicopters and several people milling around. She also saw the unmistakable outline of Thorn sitting in his powerchair, gesticulating wildly. As they drew nearer, his words became clear.

"I don't give a good flying fuck what you think. We are leaving now."

"What seems to be the problem?" Drake asked.

At the sight of Salem and his head of security, Thorn fought to regain his composure. "Our pilots here are refusing to fly despite the fact that these outrageously expensive Black Hawk helicopters are equipped with FLIR, as well as a few extras from our IT boys."

Salem watched as Drake pulled the pilots aside and spoke to them quietly. Both airmen shook their heads and pointed at the sky, seemingly refusing to change their stance.

"Well, this isn't any good," Salem said, sidling up beside Thorn. "Maybe we should call it a day."

"Maybe you should learn your place and keep your mouth shut, Miss Grainger." Thorn spat out the name, knowing how much it would rankle his target.

Salem refused to take the bait. While she found Thorn to be a pathetic creature, she also knew that he was a man that expected to get what he wanted, whenever he asked for it. She remained silent.

Bits and Bytes and the four other members of the security detail busied themselves by going over a checklist that had probably already been looked at a hundred times. It was obvious that they were going out of their way to escape the wrath of Thorn.

"I'm not paying them a penny more," the billionaire yelled in the direction of Drake and the pilots. "They are already overpaid."

Drake sauntered over to Thorn, a look of resignation on his face. "It's not a matter of money, sir. They simply refuse to fly in this fog."

"What about the equipment that Bits and Bytes delivered? That software can see through a bloody brick wall as though it wasn't there. Surely it can see through this," Thorn said throwing his arms up in the air.

The movement made the fog begin to swirl in concentric circles that spread out like waves after dropping a pebble in a pond. With each wave, the mist grew thinner, evaporating before their eyes.

Drake stared at Salem. "Are you doing this?"

Feeling her heart sink, she shook her head, the movement of her ponytail sending more of the fog drifting up and away.

"It's a miracle," Thorn said, beaming like a crazy man.

No, it's my mother," Salem muttered under her breath.

Jumping into action, Drake rounded up his team and yelled at the pilots to fire up the choppers. After surveying the sky for a moment and seeing the fog melt away, the men headed to their respective cockpits and prepared to leave.

As the fog drifted off, Salem peered out into the early morning darkness, looking in the direction of Alcatraz. She didn't need a map or co-ordinates to know the direction in which The Rock lay. Instead, she felt her mother sounding out like a beacon, calling the group to their death.

Chapter Five

As the fog rolled away, Raven couldn't help but be taken by the beauty of her surroundings. While Alcatraz was a crumbling relic held together by stories and the ghosts of the past, the surrounding area was nothing short of beautiful, especially with the rising sun painting it in shades of red and gold.

The creatures were all in place, each of them excited at the prospect of exacting revenge on their captors. Raven had warned them that Salem was off-limits, but she also knew that these were feral animals with a thirst for blood. It was her job to protect her daughter and hers alone.

Rather than go back up to the highest level of the island, where the prison lay, Raven opted to hide out in the building closest to the dock. Had she known or cared anything about the history of her hideout, she would have known that it was where the guards and their families had resided when Alcatraz was still a functioning prison.

As she made her way through the building to a vantage point looking out across the bay, she could feel the eyes of those who had died here watch her passage. She could feel their fear and confusion, and while it pained her to see spirits trapped in such a way, Raven forced herself to focus on the task at hand.

Settling herself by a window on the third floor, she sent her thoughts out into the ether, looking for one more talk with her daughter before the fight began.

***

The helicopters flew side by side, the rays of the rising sun bouncing off the gunmetal grey exterior of the craft. Salem sat between Bits and Bytes, watching as they pecked away silently at their laptops.

The two security personnel, who had introduced themselves as Chalmers and Madison, sat on ither side of the helicopter, ball caps turned backwards on their heads and guns aimed out the open doors.

"Salem. Can you hear me?"

She flinched at the sound of the voice, louder than usual in her head. Bits grabbed his laptop, which almost fell when Salem nudged against him.

"Everything okay?" he asked, a legitimate look of concern on his face.

"I'm scared of flying," Salem lied, offering up a weak smile.

"We'll be there soon, and trust me, these things are completely safe. We see to it," Bits said, nodding in the direction of his partner.

"SALEM...PLEASE ANSWER."

"I hear you."

"You must be close. I can feel it."

Salem looked into the cockpit and out the front window of the helicopter, seeing the San Francisco skyline not too far off in the distance. *"We are close. I'm scared."*

"Don't be. I will make sure nothing happens to you, even if that means giving up my life."

"I don't want that."

"I've lived many lifetimes. I'll tell you about some of them if I make it out alive."

The conversation was interrupted by Drake's voice filling the cabin as he radioed in from the other chopper.

"Listen up," he ordered. "We are five minutes out. Soldiers, remember, tranquilizer rounds only. Salem, if there is an attack, do your thing and protect the people by your side."

Never one to enjoy being told what to do, Salem resisted the urge to flip the bird. Instead, she reached out to Raven. *"Five minutes. Be ready."*

"Bits, what is the Wenlutah's current position?"

A couple of taps on his computer later, he replied, "On the high ground, outside the prison."

"Copy that. My guess is that they'll all be there, forming a protective circle around the bitch."

"Don't call her a bitch, asshole," Salem hissed.

"We will land our chopper on the roof of the prison. You will land on the main level by the boat landing dock. It's a tight fit, but not a huge problem. Hold your position and stay in the chopper. We will come to you. Got it?"

All but Salem spoke their assent.

"Salem?" Drake said.

"Yes."

"This should be a quick in and out. We will drive them in your direction. Do what you do and take them down without inflicting injury. Am I clear?'

"Crystal."

"Keep the comms open, and good luck."

"They are landing on the prison roof, Mother. My helicopter will be down by the water."

"I'll be nearby."

Beyond the city skyline, the sun rose across the bay. Alcatraz appeared, looking calm and peaceful, a state that would not remain that way for long.

***

WHUMP WHUMP WHUMP.

The sound of the approaching helicopters reached Raven before they came into view. It wasn't until she saw the glint of metal in the sky on the horizon that she knew they were really close.

Closing her eyes, she willed her creature to remain vigilant, reminding them that Salem was off limits. They had obeyed her since their release, but the prospect of fresh blood and some revenge might change all that.

Once the helicopters flew past the main wharf on Alcatraz, Raven moved quickly, descending the stairs and heading for the main entrance of the guard quarters. There were limited places for the helicopters to land, and she wanted to be as close as possible to the one that carried her daughter.

***

"Circle the island," Drake said, signaling both pilots. "Bits and Bytes, I want to know where these fucking things are at all times."

"The Wenlutah is still by the prison. The heat signatures show two more there, plus one down by the main building on the lower level." Bits replied.

"Where's the witch?"

"Lower level."

All eyes trained on the island as they performed a slow loop.

"Police boat by the wharf. Any signs of life?" Drake asked.

"Negative," Bits replied.

Thorn moved his head from side to side, looking out though both open doors of the helicopter. "Are those bodies down there?"

Looking though a pair of binoculars, one of the guards responded. "Looks like a couple of cops torn apart and what looks to be a fucking horse."

"The Nuckelavee," Thorn whimpered. "Dead?"

"Looks to be, sir."

After one full loop and no sign of any movement, Drake sent out the order. "We will take the roof of the prison. Chopper two, take the wharf."

The pilot of Salem's helicopter watched as his partner slowly lowered onto the roof of the prison. Once it touched down, he moved around to the front of the island, cursing at the limited space available to land. "Make sure you are all buckled in. This is going to be tight."

"Shit," Bits said.

"Relax, kid. I've fit bigger choppers than this into tighter spots. I got it.

"No, you don't understand. The Wenlutah is coming, and it's coming fast."

"Where?" Chalmers asked, gripping his weapon tightly.

"Other side. Madison, she's coming directly to you."

Looking down the sight of his weapon, Madison said, "I don't see it."

"I'm telling you, she's close.

Salem looked beyond Madison and caught the movement of the creature bounding down under the cover of trees. It was unlike anything she had ever seen in her life, and she suddenly wished that she was back in her little house with Terry arguing about paint colors.

As the creature broke into the open, Madison finally saw it. "What the actual fuck?"

"What is going on?" Drake asked over the intercom.

"It looks like they are bringing the fight to us." Madison yelled as he pulled the trigger.

Chapter Six

"You should have taken us down there instead of up here," Thorn yelled. "This is a colossal fuck up, Lionel."

"With all due respect, sir, had you not come, that would have been the plan." Drake tapped the pilot on the shoulder and said, "As soon as me, Anders, and Peplow are off this chopper, you start circling again."

The pilot gave the thumbs up and prepared to lift off again.

"You cannot leave me here," Thorn protested.

"And I cannot wheel you down there; you wanted to see this shit go down; I'm going to give you the best view in the house."

The security detail jumped out of the chopper and scampered away from the blades, watching as the helicopter rose into the air.

Drake led the way, kicking in the door to the stairs leading down into the prison and directing his men to follow. "Bits, an update," Drake yelled into his wireless headset, trying to compete with the sound of the departing helicopter.

He pressed the earpiece tightly into his right ear, but the only thing he heard was static. "We need to move. I think the other group might be in trouble. Eyes open, men. I cannot confirm where these nasty fuckers are until Bits or Bytes fill me in."

They tore down the stairs, watching for any movement, hoping that the way ahead would be clear.

***

Salem flinched as the tranquilizer gun fired louder than expected. Following the path of the dart, she saw the Wenlutah dodge it in mid-stride, pressing its body lower to the ground, its grasshopper-like back legs bulging with muscles as it prepared to jump.

"Shoot that fucking ugly bitch," Chalmers screamed as he unhooked his safety harness and turned towards the Madison's side of the helicopter.

The Wenlutah sprung as the second dart exploded from Madison's gun. The shot caught it in the antlers and deflected away to safety.

Salem screamed as the creature's jaws clamped around Madison's leg. Using its front legs, it gripped onto the helicopter and began to pull itself up, its weight sending the craft into a spin.

The sound of metal-on-metal tore through the morning air as the helicopter's rear blades caught the top of the guard tower at the far end of the island.

Chalmers turned, wide-eyed, to face Salem. "Do something," he pleaded as the helicopter spun wildly, the nose beginning to point towards the wharf.

For the slightest moment, Salem felt herself caught in the grip of fear, feeling as though she was

Rebecca once more. It was the sound of the pilot screaming that they were all going to die that snapped her back.

She let loose a scream of rage and threw her hands up in the air, feeling the world around her begin to slow down.

Every little detail became astonishingly clear as her senses tuned into the slowed down surroundings.

Salem unbuckled her safety harness and did the same for Bits and Bytes. She then moved through the spray of blood that lazily drifted up from Madison's leg as it was torn loose by the Wenlutah, the crimson fluid landing gently on her face.

Moving to the front of the helicopter, she unbuckled the pilot and watched for a moment as the ground drew steadily nearer.

As she dragged the pilot into the cabin, she had time to notice Drake and his men just past the guard building, guns raised as they went after the Rake, who was on all fours in mid-stride, a cruel smile on his face as though enjoying the thrill of the chase.

Raising her hands, palms out, Salem made a pushing motion and watched as the four men went flying out of the door of the helicopter. She controlled their movement on the way down, ensuring that they landed in a safe place well away from the impending impact.

While time moved slowly, it did not entirely stop. The ground now seemed impossibly close, and in the time it had taken to get the men out, the Wenlutah had torn open Madison's belly with blood-soaked claws.

With Madison's fate sealed, there was nothing to be done but get clear of the earthbound chopper. Salem leaped out the door and drifted to the ground, moving quickly away from the aircraft and over beside her fellow passengers.

With one long exhale, the world returned to normal speed.

***

As they went through the main doors of the prison, Peplow yelled and pointed. "Right there."

The Rake came around the side of the building and made for the path leading down to the wharf. Drake fired one of his darts, but the speed at which the creature moved made it a target that was impossible to hit.

Anders shouldered his rifle and reached into his holster, pulling out a handgun.

"What are you doing, soldier?" Drake demanded.

"If you two want to try and trank that thing, go right ahead. I'm opting for Plan B."

"Those are not your fucking orders."

"Frankly, Drake, I don't give a flying fuck. Thorn can keep his money. All I want to do is get out of here alive."

Peplow made as though to follow suit, but he thought better of it. "Let's get after that thing."

Drake continued to glare at Anders, but he nodded. "You do not fire those live rounds until absolutely necessary. Let's go."

The men raced down the path in pursuit of the Rake, who appeared to be slowing down to let them catch up.

"Looks like he wants to play," Peplow said.

The men closed the gap, and as they rounded a corner that brought the wharf into view, they all stopped, mouths agape as the second helicopter crashed into the ground and exploded in a massive fireball.

Chapter Seven

"Look out," Thorn shouted.

"I see it," the pilot said, banking the helicopter out towards the bay as the other chopper collided with the guard tower. The heat from the explosion passed through the open doors for the aircraft, making the billionaire gasp for breath.

"Did anyone make it out." Thorn asked, scanning the wreckage for signs of life amid the flames.

"Not that I saw, but one of your creatures went down with it."

"Which one?"

"Some big thing with antlers. It was hanging off the side. Looked like it had a hold of one of your men."

Thorn laughed and clapped his hands like a giddy schoolboy. "The Wenlutah. Thank goodness. I have another one of those on the way."

The pilot shook his head and turned back towards the cloud of black smoke now billowing up from the ground. "That's going to draw some attention."

Grabbing his smartphone out of his pocket, Thorn punched in a number and put the phone to his ear. "You are correct. I'll buy us some time. Keep your eye on what's happening down there. Get ready to pick up and move."

***

Drake and his men were pushed backward by the force of the explosion. Peplow went down hard, exhaling loudly as his butt hit the ground.

Stumbling backward, dodged a piece of shrapnel by the barest margin. Anders and the Rake were not so lucky. A piece of the rotor blade sliced the Rake in half as the explosion lifted him off the ground. Another piece of shrapnel connected with Anders' forehead with the force of a speeding bullet, passing clean through and taking off a large chunk of the back of his head.

Drake and Peplow ran to the side of the guard building and pressed themselves against the concrete wall, hissing as more pieces of the chopper flew past them or landed by their feet.

"What the fuck?" Peplow groaned, watching as the top half of the Rake pulled itself across the ground, trying to reach them.

"To hell with that." Drake unholstered his sidearm and put a bullet through the creature's head, stopping it for good.

"What about those orders?" Peplow smirked.

"Fuck that. I'm calling Thorn's chopper and getting off this fucking rock. If that crusty old fuck wants to give me grief, I still have bullets in this gun that he can argue with."

"Count me in, brother."

***

"What happened?" Bits said, patting at his body as though checking to see if he was in one piece."

"You're safe," Salem said, staring at the wreckage of the downed helicopter.

Bytes scrambled to his feet while the pilot and Chalmers looked too dumbfounded to move.

"Something wrong, Bytes?" Salem asked. Before he could respond, she heard the answer in her head. "What did you drop?"

His eyes went wide as he dropped to his knees and began scrambling in the dirt, looking for the blocking device that had fallen from his ear when he hit the ground. "It's nothing," he said.

"Oh, it's something. It's how you are all able to block me out," Salem said, reaching down to pluck the small metallic disc from the ground. "Is this what you are after? Of course, it is."

"It's not what you think," Bytes moaned, hands raised in surrender.

Salem placed the device inside her ear.

"Mother, can you hear me?"

Silence. She removed it.

"Mother, can you hear me."

"Salem, you are alive?"

"Alive and well. Where are you?"

"I'm by the entrance to the old guard building. What about the rest of them?

"One man down from our helicopter. I saved the rest, unfortunately."

Salem turned her attention to Bytes, who was crying and begging for his life. "Why are you crying?"

"I don't want to die."

Salem laughed. "Is that what you think of me? You believe me to be some heartless bitch? I saved your damn life, so why would I kill you now?"

The pilot stood and dusted himself off. "I owe you. What do you want me to do to help?"

"Stay out of my way. Bytes, can these little devices be shut down?" Salem asked, flicking the metallic disc in his direction.

"Not without my laptop," he replied, staring at the billowing smoke from the crash.

"What about you?" Salem asked Chalmers.

"I'm going to sit the rest of this out if that's okay with you. That's quite enough weird shit for one day."

"I'll be back for you. I'm going to end this."

Salem strode purposefully back onto the wharf, heading towards the guard quarters. Anger ate at her insides, her stomach churning as she thought about what Thorn might be hiding from her. With a flick of her hand, she lifted the blazing remains of the helicopter and tossed it out into the bay.

"I see you, child."

"Who is that with you?"

"The Aswang. I fear she is the only one of my group still alive."

"You have me, too."

"Stronger together."

Salem could see her mother standing in the doorway, the hag creature by her side, sniffing the air as her barbed tongue flicked in and out.

"Yes, stronger, beautiful child. You are a vision."

As they moved to meet one another, Thorn's helicopter moved in behind Salem while Drake and Peplow came out from the side of the building, weapons raised and ready to fire on Raven and the Aswang.

Raven reached out and took the creature's hand, the Aswang instantly taking on her form.

It was enough to make Drake pause for a moment. He had no problems taking down the Aswang, but Raven was a different matter. With Thorn watching it all happen from the inside of a helicopter loaded with all kinds of ammo, he didn't like his chances of getting out alive if he played the wrong card.

Salem saw the hesitation and raised her hands, ready to take them out, only to feel a sting in her neck and two more in her back.

As she fell to the ground, she spun around and saw Chalmers with his gun still aimed at her.

"I guess I'm a liar," he said, as he fired once more.

***

"The one on your right is the Aswang, Lionel. Kill it and tranquilize the witch."

Without giving it a second through, Drake put three darts into Raven before pulling his handgun and emptying the clip into the Aswang.

The creature rolled on the ground, screaming as it changed into many different forms before settling.

"Do not approach it, Lionel. Trust me, she is quite alive. I'll take care of it in a moment."

The helicopter touched down and the pilot hustled around the craft and pulled out a ramp built into the cabin. Thorn gave him a little nod as he left the ramp in his powerchair, heading in the direction of the Aswang.

He stopped on his way and reached down to stroke Salem's hair. "Not much of a fight, little one."

Bits and Bytes and the other pilot stepped out of their hiding spot, all looking rather sheepish in the presence of their boss.

"Well, what a pleasant surprise," Thorn said.

"She saved us," Bits said, nodding at Salem. "But she also knows about the blockers."

Thorn dismissed the statement with a wave. "None of it matters now." He turned to the pilot, his expression changing from calm to furious in the blink of an eye. "What happened up there?"

"One of your precious pets attacked my chopper. We're lucky…"

"Excuse me. Your chopper?" Thorn interrupted.

"You know what I mean, you crazy old fuck."

Thorn regarded the man for a moment and then turned his powerchair back in the direction of the Aswang. From a sheath on the side of his chair, he pulled out a bolo knife and ran his finger along the blade, hissing as it drew blood.

"Lionel. One more bullet into this hideous beast, please. Oh, and one in the head for that mouthy pilot."

As the bullet tore through the flesh of the Aswang, Thorn pushed the bolo knife down between its shoulder blades. His eyes lit up as he watched her squirm, rivers of black blood flowing from the wounds. She writhed for a few more seconds before falling still, her withered body sinking in on itself.

"One more for the pilot, remember."

Drake shrugged and lifted his weapon, shooting the pilot through the head.

"Load up those bitches and come with me in the helicopter. Bits and Bytes will stay behind with your men and arrange a clean-up crew."

"What about that?" Drake asked, nodding towards the police boat bobbing by the dock.

"I've made a call. It's taken care of. Now, let's head back and get these two back where they belong. We have some work ahead of us."

Drake looked around at the mess and wondered how he was getting out alive. "Why did you kill the Aswang?" he asked.

Looking at the shriveled creature, Thorn shrugged. "Easy, really. I didn't know her long enough to have an attachment. You do know how I love all my children."

Heading back up the ramp and onto the helicopter, Thorn tapped the pilot on the arm. "As soon as we are loaded up, take me home."

Chapter Eight

Salem groaned as the fluorescent lights found their way inside her barely open eyes. Her eyelids fluttered as she rolled over and tried to block out the light. She flinched as a hand fell on her shoulder.

"Relax, it's just me."

It was a voice she immediately recognized even though she had only ever heard it in her head.

"Mother? Where are we?"

"Rest. We aren't going anywhere soon."

Salem wanted to sit up, wanted to talk to her mother, but the light began to fade, and she felt herself drifting off once again.

"Sleep, child."

***

Angling his powerchair to get a better view of the television, Thorn watched the news report, marveling at how easy it was to change the narrative.

Money was the key to controlling the world, and he had plenty of it.

On the TV, a reporter stood on a boat out in the San Francisco Bay, pointing in the direction of Alcatraz.

"Residents of the city were given an early alarm call this morning after an explosion on The Rock. Details are slim, at the moment, but it appears as though there was an incident involving the security team patrolling the island, which is set to undergo renovations. All members of the security team, as well as a pair of San Francisco police officers, and a boat pilot, are presumed dead in the explosion. We will report more details as we get them."

Thorn hit the mute button on the remote control and turned his chair around, smiling widely at Drake, who sat on a couch at the opposite end of the office.

"How much did that cover up cost?" Drake asked.

"Not as much as you might think. It pays to have people in high places in your pocket.

"All's well that ends well, I suppose."

Thorn moved behind his desk and opened his laptop, tapping on the keys and replacing the news report on the TV with his desktop. "I am just getting started, Lionel. Look at those two."

With a click of a key, Thorn activated the feed showing the cell holding Raven and Salem.

"Don't you think it's time to put those two out of their misery?" Drake asked.

The billionaire frowned at the question. "Why would you suggest something so foolish. You have seen what they can do, have you not?"

"I'm wishing I hadn't at this point. I've lost some good people."

"Replaceable people, Lionel." Thorn pointed at the TV. "Those ladies cannot be replaced. They are the source of great power, which I believe can be tapped and drained."

"And transferred to you, right?" Drake finished.

"Indeed. With money comes power, but that power is little more than a low-watt bulb compared to what is inside those two. I want what they have."

The security man stood and poured himself a drink, taking a slug before he spoke again. "Is this not something you have tried before? Look how that turned out."

Thorn shook his head. "The girl, my daughter, is the answer. Remember, Lionel, it is partially my blood that runs through her." He wheeled out into the center of the office and rolled up beside Drake. "It would be easy to suggest that she gets her powers from Raven, but is it not also possible that some comes from me?"

It sounded like the ravings of a madman, but the more Drake thought about it, the more it made sense. "The previous transfusions."

Thorn thumped the arm of his powerchair and laughed loudly. "Very astute observation. I have pieces of all of my creatures swimming in my DNA. Add the blood of my daughter into the mix, and I may just unlock everything."

Drake looked up at the television and quickly looked away as he saw Raven staring back at him, as though she could see through the screen and into his soul. He knew that her powers could not touch anyone outside, but he felt a chill, nonetheless. "She is still asleep," he said, acting as nonchalantly as possible.

"There is no rush. I think we could all use some rest, although you and I do need to talk about what happened on the island." Thorn said.

Drake swallowed down the last of the bourbon in his glass and grimaced as the liquid burned his throat. "I take full responsibility."

"Nonsense. I chose the helicopter pilots, and not particularly well, I might add. That crash set off a chain of events that you nor anyone else could have predicted, Lionel."

"Still, I lost one of my men, plus, we lost most of the assets."

"A small price to pay to get my ladies back. Think no more of it."

"Thank you, sir," Drake said. "What do you need from me next?"

Moving back behind the desk, Thorn unlocked one of the drawers and pulled out a slip of paper. "I have been in contact with our man in Portland."

"Graves?"

"The very one. He has another Wenlutah lined up and ready to ship. Have Bits or Bytes arrange the transfer of funds, and you set up the details of the transfer with Graves."

"Consider it done, sir."

Drake picked up the paper, scanned the contents, and then slipped it into his pocket. "I'll take care of this immediately."

"Do it and then take the rest of the day off. I am going to want you by my side when my medical team performs the transfusion."

Turning for the door, Drake moved to head out the office, but then paused. "Can I ask a question?"

"By all means."

"What if…what if the transfusion works? What then?"

Thorn spread his arms wide. "Then the world is my oyster."

Chapter Nine

It was strange for Raven to occupy her cell with someone else after so many years spent in solitude. That it was her daughter who lay beside her on the bed was an added bonus.

She stroked the girl's hair and thought of reaching inside her mind to see her dreams and learn more about her life. It would be easy to do, but Raven also felt that it would be a terrible invasion of privacy. Better to wait for Salem to wake and then talk. There was certainly much to discuss.

She rose from the bed, careful not to disturb her sleeping daughter, and walked over to the thick glass panel at the front of the cell. She placed her hands on the glass, turned her head, and moved her ear close, hoping to catch some sound bleeding in from outside.

There was nothing.

Raven turned around and slid to the ground, her back resting against the glass. She sat and watched her daughter sleep, amazed at how much the girl looked like her. She took great relief in seeing none of Thorn's features poke through. Having any of his likenesses show up would have been akin to seeing a tear on the canvas of a masterpiece.

Time ticked slowly past, the shallow breathing of Salem the only sound to fill the space. Even the water in the toilet tucked away in the corner of the cell had ceased to drip the way it always used to. It seemed odd to Raven that someone would take the time to fix the plumbing in the short time that she had been gone. Thorn was indeed a peculiar, little man.

She thought of the man who had fathered her child and could feel her blood begin to boil. Anger had been her downfall so many times, but Raven had failed to rein it in, choosing instead to unleash it in displays of power and strength that only ever led to trouble. Perhaps her child could teach her restraint.

Salem began to stir once more, turning over in the bed and throwing the covers off her body. "Too hot," she mumbled.

Raven went to her side and pushed Salem's hair away from her face. Feeling how hot and clammy the girl was, she moved to the sink beside the toilet and held her hands under the cold water, keeping them until her fingers went numb. Returning to the bed, she dabbed at Salem's face and kept her wet hands in place when she tried to squirm away.

Caring for anyone other than herself was something foreign to the witch, yet it felt natural now. Raven didn't believe that the girl needed her, such was her power, but she hoped that Salem would want her help. The thought of not having the child at her side now brought an almost unbearable pain to her gut.

Feeling as though her heart might explode if she continued to look at her daughter, Raven went back to the sink and wetted her hands once more.

When she turned around, Salem was sitting up in bed, staring out through the glass.

"How do you feel?" Raven asked.

"Angry, but mostly thirsty.

"I can help with that." Cupping her hands under the faucet, Raven scooped up a handful of water and walked carefully back to her daughter, determined not to spill a drop.

Salem lapped up the water and gasped as she wiped away the excess from her chin.

"More?" Raven asked.

"Please."

After two more trips, Salem raised her hand.

"That's good. Thank you."

Raven wiped her hands on her tattered dress.

"Anything for you, child."

The girl turned away, as though embarrassed at the attention. "Are we back…is this where Thorn kept you imprisoned."

"It is."

With a sigh, Salem turned and faced her mother. "How could you stand it? This place is, well, it's awful."

The witch stood and moved to the front of the cell, staring off down the long, bricked corridor. She tried to see beyond the bars of the cells that lined either side, but the creatures contained within were playing shy and lurking in the corners of their personal prisons. "I imagined killing him," she finally said.

"Thorn?"

"Yes, and whichever fools he brought with him on his daily visits. I imagined slowly stripping the flesh from their bodies or tearing off their genitals and forcing to eat. I imagined a thousand ways to torture them before killing them as they begged for mercy."

Salem pulled the blanket off the bed and wrapped it around herself, suddenly feeling very cold again.

Catching the movement in the reflection of the glass, Raven turned to her daughter. "Do I horrify you?

"No." Salem pulled the blanket tighter and closed her eyes. "Before all of this, the idea of intentionally hurting anyone would have horrified me, but Thorn is a man that is easy to hate."

Raven hung her head, her red hair dropping across her face like a blood waterfall. "It is others who have made me as I am. Their lies condemned me to a life on the run, always fearing for my life."

Salem patted the mattress beside her. "You promised to tell me about your life. Will you do it now?"

The witch sighed. "I'm not sure where to begin, or what to tell."

"Let's start with the highlights. How about that?"

"If you wish." Raven moved to the bed and sat beside her daughter, who stretched out her arm and pulled her close under the blanket."

"How about you begin by telling me your name and where you were born."

"I was born the youngest of three girls on a small house sitting on stilts. My mother died giving birth, cursing me as she drew her last breath. My father, hearing the curse believed that my mother was naming me Baba Yaga, so that is what he called me."

"When was this?"

Raven held her hands out and shrugged.

"Time means very little when you are granted so much of it. Hundreds of years. Long enough to see empires crumble and to have been both a slave and a queen."

"A queen?" Salem asked, wide-eyed.

"You won't find me in any history book. It was a short reign that ended in bloodshed. That is something that has followed me. My whole life, people have wished me dead, including my father."

"Why would he wish you dead?"

Raven pressed her thumbs into her eyes and sighed heavily. "My father would vanish for days at a time, hunting food and more often than not coming back empty handed and stinking of alcohol. He began to beat me, blaming me for the death of my mother. The truth, though, was that he turned to violence when my hair turned red. His was black as pitch, as was my mother's. I assume he believed me to be someone else's child."

Salem pulled her mother in close, feeling the pain and anger flowing out of her in a torrent. "I'm sorry."

"One time, when I was around ten or eleven, he went on one of his hunting trips and stayed away longer than usual. My sisters and I were hungry, starving. Ivanna, my oldest sister, succumbed to the hunger, and…and…"

Feeling as though she had taken a blow to the gut, Salem put her hand to her mouth and choked back a sob."

"Aniya and I had to eat. We didn't know if father was ever coming back. When he finally did, there was nothing left of Ivanna but bones." Raven shrugged off the blanket and stood, beginning to pace back and forth. "He threw himself upon me, but before he could land a blow, I threw him across the room simply by thinking about doing it. I tore him limb from limb with my mind, and my sister and I feasted for weeks."

Sitting slack-jawed, Salem wanted to tell her mother to stop, but she knew that there was no way to end it.

"Aniya grew ill shortly thereafter and passed. I gave her a proper burial. I saw no reason to inflict any more pain on her." Raven looked at her daughter out the corner of her eye. "The dead still scream."

"I don't…"

"Some men, who my father owed money, came looking for him. They found me coated in blood and eating a rabbit that I had caught in the woods. They fled and told everyone that I was eating children. More men came in the night, looking to burn down my home with me inside. No one else came after word spread about how that ended."

Salem rose from the bed and went to her mother, placing an arm around her shoulder. The witch resisted at first, but then relented and fell into the embrace. "I think that's enough for today. We have visitors."

Lifting her head, Raven looked down the hall and saw Thorn approaching, followed by Drake and two other men, all of whom were heavily armed. She hissed as Thorn wiggled his fingers in a wave. "Death is coming, little man. So...much...death."

Chapter Ten

The powerchair moved slowly down the long hallway as Thorn stopped to admire his collection, cooing and throwing treats as he passed by each cell.

"I hate that man," Salem said.

"The feeling is mutual, child."

Stopping a few feet in front of the glass, Thorn turned and said something to Drake, who tapped at a device trapped to his wrist.

The exterior sounds filled the cell, making Salem jump at clutch at her chest. Raven stood still, staring down her captor.

"Good evening. How are my two favorite ladies doing?"

The women stood in silence, both reaching out to one another to hold hands.

"How precious is that scene, Lionel? We have some family bonding going on. I wonder if Daddy is invited. What do you think?" Thorn cooed.

"I'm not sure it's a party you'd want to attend, sir." Drake replied dryly.

Thorn wheeled a little closer and stuck out his bottom lip. "You both look so very sad in there. Raven, I see your pretty dress is torn. I'll have something new ready for you when I let you out." He turned his attention to Salem. "You, my dear, are quite beautiful. Other than the hair, I do think you favor your daddy."

Salem clenched her fist, her nails digging into the palm of her hand and drawing blood. She tried to fight down the anger, but she could feel it building, getting ready to blow.

"Hmm, not very talkative today, are we. How about I take over and explain what is going to happen next. Does that sound good?"

The women remained silent.

"I'll take your silence as a yes. I'm not sure how much Mommy dearest has told you about her time here, so let me fill you in."

"I am going to kill you," Raven said.

"I'm not exactly sure how that is going to happen, dear. I do believe that ship has sailed. But as you can see, I am talking to our daughter, so if you would kindly play the dutiful wife and shut your fucking mouth, I'd be much obliged."

Drake placed his hand on the butt of his gun as Salem stepped forward, a look of pure rage etched on her face.

Thorn, unfazed, continued. "As I was saying, Salem, I have a little ritual that I enjoy partaking in with each of my guests. You might call it their thank you for my giving them room and board."

A thin trail of blood fell from Salem's left nostril, all the way down over her lips and chin before dripping onto her shirt.

The men behind Drake took a backward step, one of them turning to look back the way they had come.

"Hold your positions," Drake hissed.

"Well, would you look at that," Thorn said, pointing at Salem. "It looks like you may have already got the memo and are preparing your blood gift."

Raven tore a strip of fabric from her ruined dress and held it up to her daughter's face, trying to staunch the flow of blood.

Shrugging her mother away, Salem took a step forward, her gaze fixated on a spot in the middle of the glass. Blood flowed like a geyser from her nose, and as she blinked, more began to run from her eyes.

"Make it stop, Raven screamed."

"Not yet, dear. This is just beginning to get interesting," Thorn said. "Whatever are you trying to do, sweet Salem?"

She began to tremble, the shuddering movements of her body sending blood flying onto the glass. As it hit, a chip appeared dead center, like the mark left from a pebble striking a car windshield.

"That's not good," Drake said.

Salem shook more violently, turning the chip into a crack that looked like a lightning bolt etched into the glass.

"Sir, if she gets out, we are all fucked," Drake said, tapping the awestruck billionaire on the shoulder.

"How wonderful," Thorn whispered.

The crack stretched from corner to corner, the glass seeming to warp under the stress. Blood seeped into the break and took on a life of its own, creating smaller fissures off the main crack.

Spreading her arms wide, eyes rolled back in her head, Salem began to chant in a long dead language. The cracks spread further, like serpents rising under the call of a snake charmer.

"Hit the gas," Thorn said. "Hit it now.'

Hands trembling, Drake punched in a code and watched as the cell began to fill with a misty cloud. Raven dropped instantly, but Salem stood for a moment, staring her captors down while continuing to speak in tongues. The glass warped once more, another large crack appearing before she tumbled to the floor.

"What the fuck was that?" Drake asked.

"That, Lionel, was the key to unlocking all my powers. I need her blood. Tell the medical team that we are moving up the transfusion."

"Done," Drake responded.

"Oh and have those two moved to the new cell by the lab. "There will be no escaping that one."

The men cleared a path for Thorn as he turned his powerchair towards the exit, this time moving much faster than he did upon arrival.

As they cleared the guard station and arrived at the elevator, Drake radioed for assistance. He sure as shit wasn't about to open that cell door and move the women on his own.

Chapter Eleven

Thorn shook his head and held up a hand, stopping the man in the lab coat in mid-sentence. "Hold on, doc. Run that by me again, only this time imagine that I am a blithering idiot. Talk to me in layman's terms, if you will."

Tapping at his laptop, the doctor turned it so that Thorn could see the video, which had been paused, on the screen.

"Is this the blood tests?"

"Yes. As you already know, sir, we already have plenty of samples from Raven. We have been testing those for years, looking for a way to deliver a transfusion that will bring you the, uh, the desired results you are looking for."

"Okay, go on."

"We have only recently started testing the samples from your daughter and given that you are both the same blood type, the assumption was that her plasma would be a much better fit for you."

Sighing in agitation, Thorn said, "Are you telling me that she's not.

"No, sir, that's not what I am saying at all."

Moving his powerchair closer to the desk where the laptop sat, Thorn stared at the paused video image. "Then what is it you want to show me."

"As I previously explained…"

"Keep it simple, I'm warning you. I don't have time to listen to medical mumbo jumbo."

"Of course. One of my assistants had the idea of seeing what might happen if we combined the blood of the mother and daughter. Specifically, we were looking for some type of reaction."

"Who is this assistant?"

A young blond-haired man stepped forward with his hand raised. He looked like he had just crawled out of a dumpster, his hair shooting off in all directions and his lab coat dotted with unrecognizable stains.

Thorn gave him the once over. He thought about lecturing the kid on personal hygiene, but he decided to stick to business. "What's your name, son."

"Luke Robson, sir."

"I haven't seen you around before. Are you new?"

"Yes, sir. Dr. Bloom hired me as his intern just recently.

Thorn rolled his eyes, finding it hard to believe that some punk ass kid working for nothing would deliver a major breakthrough. "I see. And where did you get the idea for mixing the blood?"

The lab assistant adjusted his sweat stained collar and flushed a bright shade of red. "Um, from the movies, sir."

"The movies?" Thorn asked indignantly.

"Yes. Specifically, *The Thing*. There is a scene where they test the blood to see who might be harboring the alien DNA, the thought being that…"

"I've seen the movie," Thorn said. "Please just tell me what happened when you combined the two samples."

"I can show you," Bloom said, pressing play on the video.

Thorn watched his medical team going through their paces, doing God only knows what with the samples. It was all rather dull and dreary stuff until they dropped a sample of both Raven and Salem's blood into a Petrie dish.

The two drops sat in their respective spots, but as Thorn watched, they began to move toward one another before meeting and mixing. The combined blood turned from crimson red to onyx in the blink of an eye, and then shot up in the air and out of sight of the camera.

Bloom hit the pause button.

"What happened, where did it go?"

The doctor pointed up to the lab's ceiling to a large hole that looked fried around the edges.

"The blood did that? Thorn asked.

Bloom nodded. "Needless to say, we called you as soon as it happened."

The billionaire gaped at the hole and then reached out and restarted the video, watching it a few more times before pressing stop. "My God."

"My sentiments exactly, sir. The easiest way I can put it is that their blood is stronger together."

"I want units of both inside me, do you understand."

"I'm not sure that's wise. You saw the reaction. We have no idea what it might do to your body."

Thorn looked back at the hole one more time. "You let me worry about that."

At first glance, the circular cell looked like an overblown killing jar. The glass was thicker than the previous cell and completely bulletproof, tempered steel on top house a series of small pipes that could pump in air or gas, as needed.

It sat on a platform in the middle of an otherwise bare room ringed by security guards, all of whom had their weapons out, aimed at the cell.

Raven and Salem sat on the wide cot that took up most of the space. The only other item in the cell was a metal bucket serving as a toilet. The women had lost latrine rights after the incident in their previous cell.

Raven looked around the space for the umpteenth time, looking for some flaw that she could expose and take advantage of. There was nothing. She brushed her hands against her daughter's fingers, the tips of which were still stained blood red. "How are you feeling?"

"Why didn't you help me?" Salem asked.

"What?"

"The glass was breaking. If you had helped, we would be out now."

Hanging her head, Raven mumbled an apology. "It happened so quickly. Perhaps my instincts have been dulled after being a prisoner for so long."

"They weren't so dull when you broke out the first time."

They lapsed into an uncomfortable silence, both watching the door sitting opposite their cell. It looked like the entrance to a bank vault, complete with a wheel-type lock in the middle and a light overhead, which was currently a blazing shade of red.

Salem let loose a sigh and grabbed her mother's hand. "I'm sorry. I shouldn't blame you."

"No, you have every reason to. I was slow to react."

"Do you think we'll get another chance?"

"To escape?"

"Yes."

Raven turned to face her daughter. "Let me ask you this. If we did get out, what would you do?"

The question took Salem by surprise, as freedom was not something that she had given much thought in her short time as Thorn's prisoner. She shook her head. "I don't know, honestly. I'd find Terry and try and get our perfectly ordinary life back."

Raven grunted. "That's something you think you could do now that you know your powers?"

Salem thought back to the hours before her life had changed. How happy she had been with her little family. She wondered where Terry was now, feeling a knot in her belly at the thought of him being somewhere alone and afraid. Her mind then drifted to Selina and Craig, the people she thought of as her parents for her entire life. The anger she had felt at them once they revealed their true identity was now turning to grief. It hurt that she would never see them again, would never get to say a proper goodbye.

She suddenly realized just how tired she was, and looking at the blood that stained her clothes, how beaten down she felt.

"Yes, I think I could. What about you?"

"I'm tired of running and hiding. I think perhaps it's time to go on the offensive." Raven's eyes came to life as she spoke. "The world is a shitty place full of even shittier people. You and I, we could change that."

"How so?" Salem asked, beginning to feel a little afraid.

"Think about what we could do, the havoc we could cause. You, child, are so much stronger than me, but together, out there in the world, we could rule."

Salem put her hand to her mouth, snorting as she laughed. "We barely made it out alive the last time."

"How long have you known about your powers?"

"A couple of days."

"And yet you are a force of nature. Imagine what you could be with a little push from your mother. We could conquer entire nations."

Pushing away from her mother, Salem walked over to the glass and looked out at the men guarding their cell. The one's she made eye contact with placed their fingers on the triggers of their guns ready to shoot, even though they were aware that the bullets would not penetrate the glass.

Salem saw fear in the eyes of each of them, and while she felt a certain satisfaction at seeing them scared, deep inside, she knew that willfully killing hordes of humans and destroying the world she knew was not something that was in her nature.

"Do you hear me, child?"

"I do, but that is not something I want."

"Who doesn't want to use their powers to rule and conquer?" Raven asked.

"People who are good."

"I don't know any of those people," Raven scoffed.

"You know me."

The tough expression on Raven's face softened upon hearing her daughter's words.

"How about we make a deal?"

"What's that?" Raven asked.

"We use any means necessary to get out of here, after which we can figure out the future."

Standing, Raven held out her arms, inviting Salem in for an embrace. "Deal," she said.

Snuggling against her mother, Salem felt their hearts beat in perfect time. She felt the anger and frustration of the last few days begin to melt away, and it felt good. "I'll tell you one thing, though, Mother, world domination is not on the list of options."

Chapter Twelve

Drake sat in his quarters and sipped on a glass of bourbon. He swallowed the last of the alcohol, savoring the taste before setting down the empty glass.

Donning a pair of glasses, he picked up the legal pad sitting by his side and read over his resignation letter. Drake wasn't entirely sure that his job was one that required any type of traditional two-week notice, but he was a stickler for formality.

He read the letter one more time, making a couple of changes before finally feeling satisfied with the final draft. He tossed the pad aside and flipped open his laptop, opening up Word. He typed up the finished letter, printed it off, and signed it before folding it up and slipping it into his jacket.

Drake wasn't sure how Thorn would react to the resignation, or whether he would even let him out alive. Drake knew where all the bodies were buried and had enough dirt on Thorn to ruin the man or to blackmail him for a ridiculous amount of money. He has no inclination to do either of those things. The truth was that if he tried to incriminate his boss, he would be opening up a can of worms for himself. Drake also had more than enough money to live a very decent life for the rest of his day. Getting out now was all about survival.

He had always believed Thorn to be borderline insane, but the man's obsession with his daughter was particularly disturbing to Drake. He also had to admit that he was more than a little afraid of the girl, afraid of what she might do when she found out about her boyfriend. Drake wanted no part of any of that.

Refilling his glass, Drake leaned back on his leather couch and closed his eyes. Sleep did not come often because that usually meant that nightmares followed. That time, though, it came easily enough.

***

The powerchair whirred quietly as Thorn followed Dr. Bloom around the large surgery as he droned on about the dangers of the upcoming transfusion. Thorn tuned him out and thought about how he would feel once the blood of Raven and Salem flowed through his veins.

He interrupted the doctor, who was in the middle of a lecture about the different blood types. "Are you sure you can keep the girls under for the duration of the transfusion? My girl is a little feisty."

"Not a problem at all, sir. You bring them to me knocked out, and I'll make sure they stay that way until the procedure is complete."

Thorn grinned as he left the operating theater, believing it would be the last time he left the room under the power of anything other than his own two feet.

***

When Salem awoke, the first thing that she noticed was the lack of guards. The room was not completely empty, but the large security team was down to two men, who hopped to attention when she sat up in the cot.

She shuffled over to the bucket and stared down the two remaining men. "A little privacy please."

The men glanced at one another, trying to make a decision. When Salem dropped her camo pants and squatted over the bucket, they turned away, the younger of the two looking suitably embarrassed.

Her business done, Salem returned to the bed and sat down facing the door, waiting for the red light to turn green. She didn't have to wait long.

Salem nudged her mother as the wheel on the door began to spin, the light changing color moments before the door swung open, revealing Thorn, Drake, and the rest of the security team.

Sitting up, Raven rubbed at her eyes and scowled as she caught sight of the group. "He's so fucking smug. I can't wait to wipe that smile off his face.

"Good morning, ladies. You won't know it from your current location, but it's a beautiful day. One might say a perfect day for an awakening."

Drake listened to the man talking and frowned, unconsciously touching his jacket to make sure that the resignation letter was still there.

Thorn maneuvered his chair to the edge of the platform upon which the cell rested, a pair of guards walking alongside. "Would you like to take a shot at breaking the glass before I tell you what is going to happen today?"

"I'm saving my strength, so I can break you," Salem said, a look of fierce determination etched on her face.

Ignoring the jab, Thorn pointed to the roof of the cell. "In a couple of hours, we will be delivering another round of gas that will have you both napping like babies in seconds. Once that is complete, you will be transported to my medical team down the hall, where I will have your blood pumped into my veins. I shall be reborn."

"What about us?" Raven asked.

Thorn pondered the question, circling the cell as he sought the answer. "I do enjoy having you both in my life, but I'm not sure I need you. If the transfusion works as expected, I may have to bid you both farewell.

"Then you had better hope that your gas and your medical team can keep me under because I am not going down without a fight."

"I do so love your spirit. I shall miss it." Thorn wheeled away and motioned one of the guards to open the exit door. "If you'll excuse me, ladies, I'm off to see a man about a Wenlutah."

They watched him go, cursing him as the light above the door turned from green to red.

"Any plans?" Raven asked.

Salem looked up at the vents blowing in the air. "I don't know. Maybe. Tell me what you think about this?"

***

Drake jogged up beside the powerchair and placed his hand on his boss' shoulder. "Can we talk?"

"Can it wait?" Thorn sighed.

Reaching into his jacket, Drake handed over the letter. "Not really, no."

The billionaire quickly scanned the page, looked up at the ceiling, and then read it again. "Is this some kind of joke, Lionel."

"No, sir. That clusterfuck on Alcatraz made it clear that I'm not the man I used to be. I'd rather walk away while I still have the chance."

"When do you want to leave?"

"Immediately, sir."

Thorn tucked the letter between his leg and the side of the powerchair. "That's not going to happen, I'm afraid. I want you there for the procedure. After that, you are free to go."

Drake was stunned, expecting an outright refusal or a bullet in the head. "I can recommend a replacement if you wish."

"That won't be necessary, Lionel. I'm thinking of asking that Graves fellow to come on board. No offense, but he strikes me as a tad more ruthless than you. That may be what I need going forward."

"Do you still want me to handle the Wenlutah transfer with Graves?"

"No, I'll do it. Tell the doctors to prepare for the transfusion and then wait until it is complete. I'll put a little something in your bank account as a thank you for being a loyal servant."

"Thank you, sir."

Thorn sped off without saying another word, his security detail jogging beside him.

Drake watched them go before seeking out Bloom. The sooner they got this shit over with, the sooner he could get out of town.

Chapter Thirteen

Salem kept one eye on the door and another one on the overhead vents. Given the speech that Thorn had given on his earlier visit, she believed the chances of him popping in again were slim. The more likely scenario was that they would drop the gas without giving any prior notice.

She twirled the two pieces of fabric from her mother's dress into balls, rolling them around between her thumb and forefinger as she waited, each second ticking by ever so slowly.

Raven lay on the cot, her breath shallow, her eyes glazed over as she kept her eye on the vents.

"Are you ready?" Salem asked. She almost posed the question again before noticing the very slightest of nods from her mother.

Without warning, the light above the door turned green while a hissing sound echoed around the cell from overhead.

"Do it," Raven said.

Salem sucked in her breath and closed her eyes, feeling everything begin to slow down. Once she felt it go as slow as she could make it, she opened her eyes and pushed the pieces of fabric as far into her nose as they would go.

On the cot, Raven's lips were pursed as she sucked in the air from within the cell. The wisps of gas formed little funnel clouds that drifted lazily down to her mouth and nose, disappearing as they got there.

Salem's eyes watered and despite her best efforts, she could feel the gas beginning to do its thing. She slowed her breathing even further and fell to the floor as she returned the world to normal speed.

She felt as though she were on the brink of a deep sleep, the voices from outside the cell echoing and seeming to come from a great distance. She felt weak, but not completely out of it, which was exactly where she wanted to be.

Through narrowed eyes, she saw Drake standing with men in lab coats, all of them wearing gas masks.

"They are out. Cleanse the cell," Drake called out in a voice that seemed impossibly deep and distorted.

The men moved around like shadow people seen during sleep paralysis, opening the door to the cell and loading Raven onto the gurney. For a moment, Salem felt as though she were floating, but she was still with it enough to know that she was being carried.

She willed her heat to remain slow and steady, her breathing shallow, as they wheeled her down the corridor to the operating room. It felt as though she were being pushed through water, and it became difficult to stay awake. Some gas had leeched into her system and was doing its best to put her under. She fought to stay as alert as possible, hopefully enough to do some damage.

***

Thorn sat up on the bed and watched as wheeled in the witch and his daughter. He was struck by how beautiful they both were and imagined what life might be like if they were a normal family unit. He was not a man prone to sentimentality, so he quickly cast the notion aside.

His thoughts turned to Drake and his resignation. Thorn knew that he should have the man killed, but what was the point? There were a hundred Drakes out there, ready to obey and kill for their share of the almighty. Graves had already accepted the position of head of security and would begin with the delivery of the Wenlutah. It was shaping up to be a very good day.

Thorn's train of thought was broken by Bloom, who placed a hand on his shoulder. "Are you ready, sir?" he asked, his voice muffled by a surgical mask.

Looking at the gurneys on either side of him, Thorn looked closely at the two women. "They are out?" he asked.

"Like a light, sir. We will continue to monitor their vital signs and administer anesthetic as needed."

"What do you need from me?"

"Just lay back and relax," Bloom said, lowering the bed to horizontal using a remote. "You are going to feel a little pressure on your arms. That's just the needles being inserted. Can I offer you a light sedative?"

"Do I look like a child at his first dentist visit? No sedative, doc. I want to be awake for this."

Closing his eyes, Thorn relaxed and listened to the sounds of his medical team at work. Try as he might, sleep came, and he drifted off."

***

"Mother, can you hear me?"

Salem sent out the signal, but she knew it was weak, knew that Raven was not receiving. She could feel her strength ebbing away and for the first time since Thorn's people arrived at her house, she felt real fear.

She could feel her heart rate begin to climb, and she fought to control it.

"Keep an eye on the young one. Hear rate is fluctuating," Bloom said.

"Should I deliver the anesthetic?"

She heard people move around the gurney, checking the machines hooked to her arm. *Slow, slow, slow.*

"Looks like a blip. She's out. Hold the anesthetic for now," Bloom said.

Rolling her head slowly to the side, Salem opened her mouth and allowed a trail of drool to escape, trying to lend to the illusion that she was completely out for the count. She cracked her eyes open and took in as much as possible although it looked as though she were seeing her surroundings underwater.

A plastic tube led from her arm to a large glass container sitting above Thorn's bed. A similar tube led from her mother's arm while a pair of tubes were hooked up to Thorn.

"Are we ready?" she heard the doctor say.

"Whenever you are," another voice responded.

"Then please begin."

Salem felt a pinching sensation on her arm and then saw her blood begin to flow up the tube and into the glass container, mixing with that of her mother.

The mixed blood swirled inside the container, turning from red to a deathly shade of black. Salem felt the floor begin to vibrate as the doctor opened a valve that allowed the ichor to run free into the veins of Thorn, whose good eye shot open and began to turn black.

Salem breathed in and out slowly, turned her head to the other side of the bed, and focused on Drake.

"Let's see what's inside that head of yours."

Chapter Fourteen

As soon as the vibrations began rippling through the concrete floor, Drake thought about making his exit. Before he could leave, though, he felt a buzzing in his left ear that turned into a high-pitched whine. He looked over to Bits and Bytes, who sat in the far corner of the room recording the procedure, but he failed to catch their eye.

The whining intensified until it became unbearable. Reaching into his ear, he plucked out the blocking device and held it between his thumb and forefinger. It looked the same as it always did. The whining stopped but was immediately replaced by an invasion of a different sort.

Drake looked at the gurney and saw Salem's eyes fluttering. "Fuck,' he managed to say before she wormed inside his head.

***

Now that she knew there was a device in place to keep her out, Salem found it easy to bypass it. She wanted to scream for joy when Drake took it out, but she focused on the task at hand, which was to find an energy source that would bring her out of her fugue state. Hate was a great source of energy, and she figured that Drake had plenty to spare.

She wasn't wrong.

Salem slipped inside his head and accessed a lifetime of memories. She saw wars and bloodshed, savagry and pain, all delivered by Drake's hand. She flipped through his catalog of atrocities, sucking in the hate of the man and the fear of his victims, all of it fueling her and making her stronger.

She wormed in deeper, flipping the memories faster and faster, so much so that she almost passed the most important of all. Reaching back, she saw Drake step out of the car, saw him walk behind Terry and Craig and saw him put bullets in the back of their head.

All pretense of unconsciousness ended at that point.

Salem let loose a scream as she pulled the needles from her arms, her blood still leaking from the holes. She stayed inside Drake mind as she leaped off the gurney and went to stand before him.

She heard guns cocked and fingers falling on triggers. They became nothing more than a hollow echo as she slowed the world down and stood before Drake, whose face was carved in a rictus of fear.

"You should be afraid," Salem whispered in his ear before making the mark of the cross on his body and turning back to take in the rest of the room, swatting away the bullets that moved slowly through the air.

It was then that she noticed Thorn standing on his bed, moving at normal speed as he tore the mask away from the ruined side of his face, which was now reptilian in appearance.

"Say hello to Daddy," Thorn said, flicking out a barbed tongue that split down the middle and

116

went off in different directions, as though possessing a mind of its own.

Salem looked beyond the billionaire, who was continuing to evolve before her eyes, to try and see what was going on with Raven. Her mother was still out cold, the excess gas she consumed keeping her under.

A scream echoed around the room as bone tore free of Thorns skull. On one side of his head, a horn, like that of a bull broke lose while a half rack of antlers burst free on the other side.

Deciding that it was time to speed things up again, Salem rose her hands to set time straight but paused for a moment when she saw muzzle flashes appear on the guns held by the security guards. In low motion, it looked as though they were holding sparklers, and Salem thought it looked almost pretty.

She followed the slow track of the bullets and saw that they were all headed to the point where she previously stood, right in front of Drake.

With a wave, she returned things to normal speed, flinching as the sound of gunfire joined in with Thorn's screams in a hellish chorus.

Salem turned in time to see Drake's body slice apart down the middle and across the shoulders in the mark of the cross she had left. Each of the pieces were torn to shreds by the hail of bullets as they fell to the ground and piled up like dead meat in an abattoir.

The guards all looked confused for a split second, wondering where their target had gone and why their leader was now nothing more than torn flesh and bones. Their training kicked in quickly though, and they all turned their weapons on Salem as she covered the space between herself and Thorn in lightning speed.

"Lay down your weapons," the billionaire yelled.

The men turned to face him and looked horrified at what they saw. Thorn was not a pretty sight at the best of times, but he was now something torn from the pages of a nightmare novel. Besides the lizard face and crown of horns, he also had gills on his neck and a torso that looked like that of a bodybuilder. His arms were sinewy and slender, ending in oversized hands ending in razor sharp claws. Thorns legs were thick and muscular with cloven hooves for feet.

Salem hit the floor and slid under Thorn's bed at the same time the guards all dropped their weapons. She came out the other side, close to Raven's gurney and stood quickly, almost ripping her skin on the spikes that jutted out of Thorn's back.

"Where are you going, little one?" Thorn asked as he jumped off the bed, his hooves raising sparks as they contacted the floor.

Never taking her eyes off the man, Salem pointed at the guards, the medical team, and Bits and Bytes, and said, "Sleep." They all dropped to the ground as she made it to her mother's side.

"You got what you wanted. All I ask is that you let me walk out of here with my mother. I won't hurt you if you do that."

Thorn looked at her for a moment, his yellow eyes flitting left and right, and then he threw back his head and laughed.

"Oh, child. Do you really believe you can hurt me now? You and I were meant to be. Don't you see that? Think of the children we could bring into this world. An unbeatable army." His tongue flicked out quickly and licked Salem's neck, leaving a trail of sticky drool.

Swallowing down the rising bile, Salem wiped her neck and shook the thick mucus from her fingers. She needed time to think. "What about Raven?"

"What about her? She is obsolete."

"Not true," Salem said. "Your transformation only came with blood from us both. You still need her."

"Looks at me," Thorn said, spreading his arms. "I am a finished work of art. I need nothing more from her. You, though, are the golden child. What wonders we will accomplish together."

Mother, please wake up. I need you. I NEED YOU."

The internal scream seemed to do the trick, as Raven's eyes began to flutter open.

Chapter Fifteen

"WAKE UP."

Thorn tilted his head to the side and narrowed his eyes. "Is that you I hear yelling, Salem?" It's faint, but I can hear something."

Pressing back against the gurney, Salem reached out and grabbed her mother's arm, sinking her nails in as deeply as they would go.

"I don't want to fight you. I want to love you as a father should."

"Fathers don't have dreams of impregnating their daughters," Salem spit back.

"Oh, I bet that Craig would disagree. I'm sure he looked at you and had some impure thoughts. What man wouldn't? You are a ravishing creature."

"Craig was more of a father to me than you will ever be. "Salem felt her mother's muscles tense under her grip, so she loosened it and moved her hand down to Raven's wrist, where she felt the pulse grow stronger."

"What can I do as a show of good faith?" Thorn asked, taking a step closer to Salem.

"Let me talk to Terry."

The billionaire turned to look at the torn body that used to be Drake and smiled, flashing a set of fanged teeth that glistened with poison at the tips.

"You did that to him? There is more of me in you than you think. I'm sure you already know that talking to Terry is out of the question."

Raven's pulse quickened some more.

"When is it all enough?" Salem asked.

"What do you mean, daughter?"

"You have money, power, everything that most people can only dream of, yet still you drain the blood and ask for more," Salem said, nodding at the needles still stuck in Thorn's arms.

With a glance at the glass container, which was about one-third full, he ripped the tubes out of his arms and let them fall, the blood dripping and pooling around his hooves. "If you join me, it will be enough.

Salem smiled demurely and walked towards her father, trying to keep his focus off of Raven, who was now beginning to sit up on the gurney. She needn't have worried, as Thorn only had eyes for her.

"You see what we can be together, child. Come to me."

Moving in close, Salem placed her hands on his bare chest and moved them slowly down to his abdomen. Thorn moaned and went to pull her in close, which was when Salem struck him in the belly with the palm of her hand, sending Thorn flying across the room, a look of surprise on his face.

Snatching up the dripping tubes, Salem pulled Raven's gurney in close and said, "Drink."

"What?" Raven asked, her voice slurred.

"Stronger together, remember?"

Without giving it another thought, Raven grabbed the tubes and shoved them into her open mouth, sucking down the contents of the glass container in a matter of seconds.

"What are you doing? "Thorn raged, picking up one of the passed-out guards and snapping his spine over his knee." He threw the body across the room and roared in frustration as Salem swatted it away with little effort.

"You are going to need to do better than that," Raven said as she hopped off the gurney. "It's two against one now."

Thorn scuffed his right hoof on the ground and leaned over, getting ready to charge. "You forget that I am many, all in one. I cannot be stopped."

Salem made to step forward, every muscle in her body coiled tight like a spring. A hand on her arm stopped her.

"This one is mine. You should leave," Raven said.

"I'm not going anywhere."

Thorn charged, tossing aside medical equipment with a wave of his hand, clearing a path to the witches.

"Together then. I'll fight, you slice."

Raven sprang forward and grabbed Thorn by the throat, covering the gills and leaving him fighting for breath.

He grabbed the witch by the arm and raked his claws along her skin, tearing open ragged wounds that healed as quickly as they opened.

As Raven continued to squeeze, Salem moved her hands as though performing karate moves, each movement through the air applying razor cuts to Thorn's flesh.

Thorn stopped scratching and instead grabbed Raven's arms, bending them backwards with a sickening crack that sent bones out though her forearms.

With a scream of pain, Raven removed her hands from around Thorn's neck and drove the jagged bones from her compound fractures into the open wounds that Salem created on his chest.

Panicked, Thorn concentrated on healing the wounds, but Salem simply moved faster, slicing at every part of his body. When she reached the

Achilles on his right leg and tore it open, he went down on one knee with a howl of agony.

"Put your hands on me," Raven yelled.

Salem moved towards her mother but was lifted from her feet and sent flying by Thorn, who pointed at the guards and brought them awake. He opened his mouth wide and sent his barbed tongue flying out and into Raven's shoulder, holding her in place as she removed the bones from his chest and began to heal.

"Shoot this fucking bitch," he demanded.

The guards opened fire. The bullets that reached Raven bounced off her as she smiled in Thorn's face. A few that missed tore through his tongue, tearing it off, leaving a wriggling stump in Raven's shoulder.

Gouts of black blood spurted from the wound as Thorn flailed and tried to make it stop. The man had all the power in the world, but he was at a loss on how to best use it. He tried to heal his wounds, but the blood loss made him weak. The scales on one side of his face began to flake off and the reptilian eye on that side turned milky white.

Salem ran to her mother, pausing only to disarm the guards with a flick of her wrist. She watched as the men bolted, the fight going out of them as they took full stock of their surroundings.

Feeling her daughter's hands on her shoulder, Raven said, "Heat."

The women closed their eyes and slowly began to raise their body temperature, warming the blood in their veins and that which ran through Thorn. As they did so, Salem continued to slice.

Blood flowed freely from Thorn and boiled his flesh as it streamed down his body. Blisters showed up on his skin, popping freely and sending little geysers of blood flying into the air, each drop bubbling and fizzing as it hit the ground.

"Enough," Raven said, as she stood and pulled her daughter away. "Maybe one more cut."

Holding out her arm, Salem slowly drew it across Thorn's body, opening a wound across his abdomen, spilling entrails that flopped onto the floor.

Thorn grabbed at his innards, trying to push them back inside his body, but his talons tore them into smaller shreds. He looked up at his tormentors, tears brimming in his eyes, and as he went to speak, the blood of the witches boiled over and exploded, tearing him into a million tiny pieces.

Salem wiped the gore away from her face and looked around the room. "I wouldn't want to be the one cleaning up this mess."

Chapter Sixteen

Salem sat behind the desk and surveyed the men before her. Bits and Bytes sat with their laptops open, eyes on her and waiting for her command. Dr. Bloom sat over on the couch, holding a folder and displaying a smug grin.

"Dr. Bloom, you have news for me?"

"Indeed, and it's good. The DNA tests have proven beyond any doubt that you are Spencer Thorn's only child, and therefore rightful heir to all his assets."

"The lawyers are drawing up the papers now, but it's a mere formality. We expect you to be fully in charge next week, not that you haven't been for the past month," Bytes said, blushing furiously.

Salem nodded. "Good. Thank you, doctor, that is all I need from you today." She watched as he left the office and closed the door before she continued.

"How goes the move?"

Bits pushed his glasses onto the bridge of his nose and began to type. "As of now, half of the creatures have been transported back to their natural habitats. That includes most of the trickier species. It should all be smooth sailing from here, so no more than another couple of weeks before they are all gone."

"Excellent. Good work. How about business, Bytes?"

"Business is booming. It's almost as though you know exactly which moves to make and when to make them." Bytes laughed.

"Funny how that works." Salem regarded both men for a moment. "I've been thinking. I don't believe we have been formally introduced. I'm Rebecca Grainger."

The IT guys looked at one another and then at the hand reaching across the desk.

"I'm Ralph Butterweck," Bits said, shaking Salem's hand.

"Harold Higginbotham," Bytes said doing the same.

Salem frowned. "Quite the mouthful. Perhaps we should stick with Bits and Bytes."

Both men grinned and said, "Yes, please," in unison.

They rose to leave, but Bytes paused. "Can I ask a personal question?"

"Of course," Salem replied.

"Where is Raven?"

Salem spun her chair around and looked out the window to the city beyond. "She's out there, taking care of business in the way she knows how. We'll see her from time to time, I'm sure."

***

Shutting out the sound of the barking sea lions, Raven turned her face to meet the sun, enjoying the warmth of the summer rays.

She sat in a wooden rocking chair outside her storefront, taking a moment to relax before the next wave of tourists arrived, desperate to know what their future held.

It was dull work, but work that served a purpose. With the death of Thorn, most of the anger and her hate fled with his soul. Still, Raven knew that the world was still a messy place. She had promised her daughter that there would be no mass killings, no revenge for a life on the run. Raven had lived up to that promise, but when the wrong person stepped into her shop and offered up their palms and their innermost secrets, she made sure that the breath they took inside her establishment would be their last.

Raven felt a shadow fall across her face and believing that the sun had gone behind a cloud, she opened her eyes. It was no cloud, but rather a massive man who totally blocked her view of the bay.

"Are you Madame Raven?" he asked in a voice that sounded as though he gargled with broken glass.

"At your service," Raven replied adopting an Eastern European accent. "What may I do for you."

The man looked a little embarrassed, hanging his head as he spoke. "I'd like to know what my future holds.

Raven probed inside his mind and saw a large circular clearing in the middle of the woods. She also saw creatures that she recognized as the Wenlutah feeding on innocent people strapped to a sacrificial altar while the man and his friends knelt in worship. "Of course, mister…?"

"Graves."

"Welcome. Please step inside," Raven said, opening the door for him.

"Thank you," he grunted.

Following him inside, Raven closed and locked the door behind her and flipped the sign from open to closed. With a smile, she dropped the accent and said, "Let's get started, shall we?"

Bonus Short Story

Alter Boys originally appeared in Infamy: A Crazy Ink Anthology. It is a twisted take on the mind of Jeffrey Dahmer. I hope you enjoy it...

I was trying to think of a way not to kill them...I wanted an indefinite effect...So I wouldn't have to go out looking for partners...That's why I tried the drill technique...So I could keep them alive, interactive, but on my terms.

- Jeffrey Dahmer

The knife was small, but its keen blade was more than up to the task at hand.

"Dude, what the fuck? That's gross."

Jeffrey ignored his friend, choosing instead to continue trying to separate the dog's head from its body. Blisters were forming on his cutting hand, and the muscles in his arm and shoulders throbbed like a rotten tooth.

"Are you listening to me, man?" the gangly kid hollered, his voice cracking under the strain of puberty's grasp.

The thought of leaving the dog and moving on to larger prey flashed through his mind, the whiny nature of his friend's voice cutting through his calm exterior like a bullet to the brain. Jeffrey turned to tell the boy to shut up, but when he did so, he saw that the world around him was changing. His friend was gone, and the trees were twisting and warping, as though the surrounding landscape was being seen through a kaleidoscope.

Jeffrey gave his head a little shake, the effort of doing so, sending tiny particles of sweat flying through the air in slow motion. He could clearly see them go, each droplet awash in the colors of the rainbow. They looked like the wings of a fly seen up close; beautiful yet vile, all at once. The world continued to slow down, tilt, and shift, bringing with it a wave of nausea that forced Jeffrey to swallow hard and focus on his breathing.

"It's not happening, it's not happening," he said aloud.

When he opened his eyes once again, the forest was at a standstill, but a clearing had opened up. He imagined it to be how things would look if a tornado had torn through the woods and uprooted the trees and surrounding foliage, cutting a swathe where nothing would ever grow again. Perhaps the spinning had been real, but would he not have heard or felt the storm coming before it hit and laid waste to such a large portion of the woods?

Unsure of what to do, Jeffrey stood and, forgetting all about his current science project, took a few tentative steps in the direction of the barren space, now noticing that a bright light was starting to pulse within the gap. He used his arm for shade as he moved closer, but the glow seemed to find a way through, the intensity of its glare sending a jolt of pain shooting across his forehead and down behind his eyes. He wanted to turn away, but it was then that he noticed a silhouette emerging from the light, the figure seemingly beckoning him forward. Ignoring the pain, Jeffrey forged ahead, determined to find out the identity of the man inside the radiant glow.

It did not take long for the outline to fill in, the details creating an image that was all too familiar to him.

"Dad? What are you doing here?"

The man said nothing in response. Instead, he stepped to one side, pointing in the direction of the light and suggesting that Jeffrey continue on.

"My head hurts, Dad. Don't make me go in there."

His father remained still like a statue, unblinking, and continuing to point in the direction that he wanted his son to go. Glancing backward, Jeffrey could see the world behind him begin to shimmer and fade, leaving him no choice but to continue onwards. Two more steps took him through the light and into another space that was all too familiar—his parent's bedroom.

The curtains, which were thick and heavy, were drawn, making it tough to make out any precise details. It was even harder for Jeffrey to get his bearings given that his eyes were still adjusting to the gloom after being assaulted by the harsh exterior light he had just borne witness to. He turned to speak to his father, but found himself alone, a battered set of drawers and some tattered wallpaper having filled in the gap he has just passed through.

Disoriented and a little afraid, Jeffrey quickly turned his attention back to the center of the room, the sudden movement bringing another sharp jolt of pain to his forehead. He stood still, allowing the cranial shock wave to pass while also allowing his eyes to adjust. It took a moment, but when everything was clear again, he could see that someone was swaddled in blankets in the middle of the double bed that took up a large part of the space in the bedroom. The covers rose and fell slowly, a sure sign that whoever the occupant was, they were caught up in peaceful slumber.

He moved closer to the bed, beginning to pick up the rhythm of the breathing and the small moans coming from the sleeper. The scent in the room was also beginning to tickle his nostrils. The faint aroma of potpourri was being overpowered by something a little stronger. Jeffrey had tortured and killed enough animals in his time to have become intimately aware of the scent of approaching death. Once he caught a whiff of that, he knew that it was his mother who was before him.

"Is that you, Jeffrey?"

He was so caught up in his own thoughts that he was startled by the sound of his mother's voice slashing through his silent reverie. "Yes, Mom, it's me," he said, heart racing.

She pulled back the covers a little and turned to face her son, her pallid skin hanging in folds and distorting in the limited light available in the room.

"Lean closer. Let me see you."

Jeffrey did as he was told, leaning forward until he was just inches in front of her face. He did not receive the reaction he was expecting, as his mother recoiled slightly, letting out a little gasp, her open mouth squeezing out a short blast of fetid breath that confirmed her sickness. "What have you done. Jeffrey? I see blood on your hands and darkness in your heart," she croaked.

Remembering the dog, he looked down at his hands, a little embarrassed, but he was surprised to see that they were clean and free from any incriminating evidence.

"A mother knows, Jeffrey."

"There is nothing to know. I…"

"A mother knows, and I am sorry for my part in where you are. A boy needs attention and lots of it. I've been sickly for as long as I can remember and that has hurt you. Perhaps worst of all, I have demanded your father's attention, taking even more of it away from you. Wickedness finds a way into the hearts of boys whose whims are left unchecked. Do you understand?"

Jeffrey looked at his mother, seeing a strong woman for the first time in his life. "I think so," he said.

"There is still time for you, Jeffrey, but you are now of an age when decisions need to be made. There are two distinct paths that you can follow. The one you are on now can be broken. It just requires you to hop on over to the other path. I'm sure you will still be able to see it if you look hard enough."

He wasn't sure what to say to that. He had never thought about where his life was taking him, choosing instead to go with his gut. He still believed that decisions made now would have no bearing on his future, but he soon felt forced to think about where he might end up. Just as he was about to respond to his mother, Jeffrey heard a voice from outside calling his name.

"Ignore it, Jeffrey. Stay with me," his mother pleaded.

He tried, but the voice sounded angry and insistent. Like the light from before, it also hurt his head, a ribbon of pain tied tightly from front to back and top to bottom. Stepping over to the window, he pulled back the curtains, his mother imploring him to stop. "Come away from there, Jeffrey. Ignore that kerfuffle and come sit with me, please."

The sound of his mother's voice was like a bone saw ripping through his skull, adding to the immense pain that he was already feeling there. He pushed her voice as far into the background as possible as he pulled back the curtains and looked down into the back yard. A man stood there, clad in an orange jumpsuit, clutching a metal pipe in one hand and some tattered piece of paper in the other. The man was screaming loudly, but the only word that Jeffrey could decipher was his name, which he repeated like a mantra.

It was clear that the jumpsuit-clad individual was filled with evil intent, yet Jeffrey felt no fear. Instead, an air of invincibility surrounded him as he looked down at the man from the second-floor bedroom window. "I am above him; I am better than him," he whispered.

While it would have been impossible for the man to hear those words, he flew into a rage, swinging the metal pipe wildly and screaming, "DAHMER," at the top of his lungs as soon as they left Jeffrey's lips. As the man raged, the sun broke from behind the clouds; it's golden rays catching the metallic frame of an old swing set sitting in the yard. The reflection hit Jeffrey in the eyes with the force of a supernova, driving him back from the window, palm pressed against his forehead as another wave of pain struck. Before reeling backward, though, he saw uniformed men bolting out of the woods behind his parents' property, seemingly intent on tackling the strange, yet somehow familiar, yelling man in the backyard.

"It's time to choose, Jeffrey," his mother croaked, pointing to the wall directly in front of her bed.

He turned and was surprised to see a pair of doors standing before him, entries that had never been there before. The first of them was white, its paint chipped and peeling, scuff marks from errant shoes staining the bottom like puck marks on the boards at a hockey rink. It stood in stark contrast to its neighboring door, a brilliant black monolith that seemed to suck out all light from its surroundings and throw it back in the form of the reflection of anyone who dared stare into its dark heart.

Jeffrey found himself caught in a trance, feeling the door pull him closer as the darkness oozed from its very being. As he stepped closer, he began to see his own reflection, but it was not as he looked now. The person staring back was older, more handsome, and a million times more confident looking than young Jeffrey currently felt on any given day. He instinctively knew that this was his older self and he liked it, a little smirk playing across his lips as the reflection beckoned him forward.

"There is no way back from that one," his mother said, her voice becoming weaker and more distant with each word.

He looked back at his mother one last time before grasping the onyx handle and stepping into snow and ice covered streets in the heart of Milwaukee. Jeffrey shuddered as a cold winter wind blasted his body, the jacket he was wearing doing little to hold out Mother Nature's icy fingers. It took a moment for him to get his bearings, but once he did, he knew that this was a place where he could go to get out of the cold.

Sitting across the street was a nondescript looking building that could have been mistaken for an abandoned structure were it not for the purple light shining above a dark doorway. Jeffrey knew better, though; he knew it as a fertile hunting ground, the place to go to sate his ever-growing need for power and control. The bar was home to willing sheep, and he the shepherd, ready to tend to his flock.

Jeffrey shuddered, more from the prospect of the hunt than from the cold that crept inside his clothes and goose fleshed his skin. Excitement took hold, yet he remained calm on the outside as he crossed the street and shouldered open the door of the bar. The exterior cold was pushed back by the warm glow permeating from inside the bar. Cigarette smoke hung in the air, adding a fresh patina of nicotine stains to the already browned-out light bulbs. The years of smoke damage meant that the lighting in the bar was always dim, the ideal cover for a hunter on the prowl.

Heads turned as Jeffrey stepped inside and strode confidently toward the bar, the server giving him a little nod of recognition as their eyes locked. In the background, the jukebox played "Cut's Like a Knife," by Bryan Adams, the appropriateness of the song making Jeffrey smile as he ordered his scotch. The first sip of the amber liquid sent a bloom of warmth through his chest, bringing a contented sigh that made him forget, for just a moment, about the pounding pain that still battered his brain in a relentless wave.

"You smell like chocolate, handsome. Do you like chocolate?"

Lost in the senses that the scotch brought to life, Jeffrey hadn't noticed the man sit down beside him at the bar. He was annoyed that the sound of the visitor's voice made him jump a little, as those moments made him feel weak. Displeased, Jeffrey turned to put his uninvited guest on blast, but he was given pause when he set eyes on him. The man was young, albeit legal drinking age, and he was possessed of the most gloriously perfect skin that Jeffrey had ever laid eyes on. His flesh was the color of mocha and free from any distinguishing marks. The wispy goatee that the man wore may have looked ridiculous on anyone else, but on his face, it was perfection. Jeffrey shuddered once more as he thought about how those fine hairs might feel when brushing against his naked body.

The man was smiling adoringly, obviously infatuated with Jeffrey and obviously awaiting an answer to the question that he had just asked. "I do like chocolate, especially when it is sweet and ready to eat. What's your name?"

"Ricardo," the young man replied, fanning himself daintily with his hands, suddenly looking demure in spite of his initial bold advances.

Another blast of pain hit Jeffrey square on, but he shrugged it off, blotting it out as he drank in every square inch of the beautiful creature before him. "Are you sweet, Ricardo?"

"I'm as sweet as you want me to be, honey."

"Drink with me. I want to know some more about you before we get to the tasting. What do you say?"

"Oh, I like that idea," Ricardo cooed. "Are you going to tell me your name?"

"Not yet. Drink," Jeffrey said, sliding a fresh glass of scotch in the direction of Ricardo.

The young man took a tentative sip, the grimace on his face a clear sign that the peaty beverage was not his usual drink of choice. Jeffrey enjoyed the moment, as it showed that perhaps Ricardo might be compliant and ready to play the game that was in store for him. Giving him another full once over, Jeffrey saw his prey as potentially being the one. Sure, there had been others like Ricardo in the past; pretty little things willing to do anything when first asked, but who all failed to pass the final test. They were all a disappointment, though they did continue to serve in another capacity. A man has to eat, and they were all delicious in their own way.

"I don't recall ever seeing you before, Ricardo. I'm sure I would have remembered someone as beautiful as you. Is this your first visit?"

The fanning continued, Ricardo's skin tone taking on a darker hue as he flushed from the flattery.

"Yes, it is. I've…I've heard about this place," he stammered, "But it's the first time I've dared venture in."

Jeffrey smiled. "Aren't you glad you stopped by?"

Ricardo took another tug on the glass, seemingly warming to the taste of the liquid with each sip. "I am glad, but it wasn't easy for me to take the step. No-one knows my nature although there aren't that many people in my life at this point."

"Oh, why's that?" Jeffrey prodded.

The young man sighed, his shoulder slumping. "My mother abandoned me at birth, sending me into the system, which churned me up and spat me out. The other boys in the group homes I lived in were rough and ready, whereas I was shy and meek. They could smell the fear on me, beating me and calling me a fag on a daily basis. They would say such mean thing, but all so true, as though they could look inside me and see my soul."

Jeffrey's heart raced as the story unfolded. Where pity and empathy should have reigned, opportunity thrived. It was a gift; it had to be. This man had been sent to fulfill the dream that Dahmer so desired; he could feel it. "Surely, you must have made some friends?" he asked.

"Not really, not anyone that you would call close. I've had some flings, but never a steady boyfriend. I do enjoy the company of strangers, though, which is why I just had to come to talk to you. I never expected to see someone as stunning as you in a place as devoid of light and life as this, this shithole."

"It's my chocolate scent that draws them like flies. Delightful little creatures all looking for me to melt in their mouth."

Ricardo gasped, before licking his lips and saying, "Do you want to get out of here?"

As much as Jeffrey wanted to get started, he forced his heart rate and breathing to slow down, trying to get himself back in control and on the path to glory.

"I do," he said, "But let's take a moment. I want to learn a little more about you. I am somewhat selective, and while you check a lot of my boxes, I need to know more."

Just as those words left his mouth, pain once again hit him hard, doubling him over on the barstool before forcing him to bolt upright with a shot to the temple.

"My God, are you alright?"

"I'm fine, Ricardo. It's a migraine, nothing more. This will pass, trust me."

Jeffrey ordered another round, flashing a pair of digits at the bartender as he spun his hand, the universal symbol for another round. He could feel Ricardo's eyes on him, studying him warily. He could also sense that he was about to lose him if he couldn't get the pain under control. His breath hitched as another minor tremor shot across the back of his head, but the scotch and the presence of his now welcome guest served as a fast-acting painkiller.

Wiping away tears from a rheumy right eye, Jeffrey said, "All better now. Come on, drink up, and let's talk about what we might do tonight."

Jeffrey could see Ricardo's doubts wash away after flashing him a smile and placing a hand gently on the young man's leg, his fingers playing an oh so delicate piano solo on his upper thigh.

"There is something you should know about me, Ricardo, before we go any further."

"Tell me, please."

"I like to be in control. I like to call the shots and be fully satisfied. How do you feel about that?"

The young man flushed again, flustered, yet also excited. Jeffrey could feel that excitement as he moved his hand a little further north on Ricardo's leg. "You look like a God. I will gladly lay before you as a willing servant. What should I call you?"

With the deal done and the true nature of the game about to commence, Jeffrey smiled and said, "God will suffice quite nicely."

Tossing more than enough money to cover the drinks on the bar, Jeffrey took Ricardo by the hand and led him towards the exit. As he turned to urge him on, he was once again struck by a brutal blow, the force of which sent him staggering forward into the door. As he lifted his head to try and get his bearings, he found himself, Ricardo still in tow, standing in front of a different door, this one adorned with corroded numbers reading 213.

"You must be a little tipsy from that scotch, my beautiful God. I know I am."

Jeffrey rested his forehead on the door, the coolness of the wood bringing with it a modicum of relief. He certainly did feel woozy, but he thought it had more to do with the pain and the sudden perspective shifts than the liquor. He knew how to handle his alcohol and was aware that a few fingers of liquid fire would not leave him feeling this out of sorts.

"You might be right," he lied, slipping the key into the lock and opening the door.

Reaching inside the door, Jeffrey flipped on the light and invited Ricardo to step inside.

"Not to be rude, but it smells a little funky in here," Ricardo said, pinching his nose in an attempt to keep the odors out.

"My apologies. I've been working double shifts at the chocolate factory and have fallen a little behind. I'll bet there's an old pizza box hiding under the couch."

Ricardo faltered, seemingly unwilling to step any further into the apartment. He flinched a little as Dahmer touched his shoulders and started to massage, placing a gentle kiss on his neck for good measure.

"Relax," Jeffrey said. "I promise, I'll make you forget all about that smell soon. Do you really want an old pizza slice to ruin a fun night?"

"Hmm. If your hands are as wonderful everywhere else as they are on my shoulders, then pepperoni be damned. I think it's time we moved straight to the chocolate dessert."

Steering him into the apartment and kicking the door closed behind them, Jeffrey spun the young man around and kissed him. He could taste the malty flavor of the scotch on his tongue, a not unpleasant sensation that got the juices flowing. It was the thought of what was to come soon that really heightened his passion, though, but he knew there was work to be done before the final test was administered.

"Have a seat, and I'll get us a drink," Jeffrey said.

A look of disappointment flashed across Ricardo's face, which quickly turned into a petulant little pout. "I'd sooner eat first and drink later," he said, adopting a childlike affect that tested Jeffrey's powers of control.

"You'll get to eat soon enough, but I've had a long day at work and could use another drink to loosen up completely. You did say you would do whatever your God asked of you. This isn't a sign of defiance, is it?" Jeffrey smirked.

Ricardo bowed in mock deference, waving his right hand as though doffing some foppish headwear. "Your wish is my command, good sir."

Motioning his guest to have a seat, Jeffrey headed into the kitchen and pulled out a cheap bottle of scotch. He has better bottles in his collection, but those were being saved for special occasions. Dropping in a couple of ice cubes and a liberal splash of the hard stuff, he added a small sachet of powder into Ricardo's drink and stirred it with his finger before heading back into the living room and offering up the tainted alcohol. He was a little dismayed to see Ricardo place the glass on the table and pat the space beside him on the sofa. Thinking quickly, despite the pain in his head, Jeffrey said, "What shall we drink to?"

"Hmm, let me think," Ricardo replied, scooping up the glass and running hid pinkie around the rim. "How about we drink a night to remember?"

"I can get behind that. Cheers." Jeffrey gave a quick air toast and slammed back his scotch in one gulp. Sensing that this was a signal that the fun was about to begin, Ricardo did the same, the effects of the drink, causing the room to spin a little as he jumped to his feet.

"Steady."

"Oh, that one caught me all funny. I'm not used to drinking hard liquor," Ricardo slurred.

"I hope you can handle other hard things, though," Jeffrey said, taking his guest by the hand and leading him to the bedroom.

The room was veiled in darkness, the meager glow from the streetlights barely penetrating windows that were rimmed with winter frost. As Ricardo sat on the bed, Jeffrey went over and pulled close the drapes, switching on a small bedside lamp in the process. Once again, he saw the raving man in the orange jumpsuit on the street outside, shadow people approaching him from countless different directions. The low watt bulb offered little in the way of light, but it was enough to allow Ricardo to get a full view of the furnishings in the cramped space.

"What is all this stuff," he asked, motioning towards a pitch-black table flanked by a blue plastic barrel on one side and a full skeleton on the other.

"That's my workbench and soon to be an altar," Jeffrey replied, as though it were the most reasonable response in the world.

"Are those…are those skulls? Are they real?"

Before he could respond, another phantom blow caught Jeffrey in the temple, the force of which sent him reeling like a drunk at closing time.

"I need to know if those are real," Ricardo pleaded, his legs giving out on him as he tried to stand.

Jeffrey placed his hand on the table and tried to steady himself, wondering for a moment if he had taken the drink that was laced with drugs. It wasn't until he saw Ricardo struggle to move that he realized his own issues were coming from somewhere else.

Those issues were put on the backburner as Jeffrey composed himself and grabbed Ricardo by the collar as he tried to crawl out of the room. The young man tried to fight, kicking his legs as though riding an imaginary bike, but the sedative was beginning to kick in, making it easy for Jeffrey to drag him over to the table and lift him up onto it.

Ricardo's eyes were beginning to roll back into his head; the whites shot through with rivers of red branching out in a million different directions. Jeffrey wanted him to see all that was going on, with a rough slap to the cheek snapping the eyes back into orbit.

"You are going to listen to your God, am I right?"

Ricardo looked up at his captor, pupils dilated, and said, "What are you doing to me?"

"Tell me you are still compliant. Tell me that you are still willing to do anything I ask. If you can do that, we can start moving towards a glorious life together. Can you do that for me?"

Tears rolled lazily down Ricardo's cheeks, terror, mixed with the sedatives, making it impossible for him to speak. He nodded.

"Good. Then we can begin."

Reaching into his pants, Jeffrey removed the pocketknife that had served him so well all those years ago. He was sure that he had lost it as a kid, so was a little surprised to see it there, the blade as sharp as ever. With practiced movements, Jeffrey cut away the buttons of Ricardo's shirt, pulling back the fabric to reveal a smooth, hairless chest that looked perfect in every way.

"Beautiful," he whispered as he leaned over and flicked his tongue over the young man's nipples. Moving on, he placed gentle kisses all over the torso, slowly but surely making his way down to the navel, a snail trail of saliva in his wake. Wispy black hairs as soft and delicate as those on Ricardo's face, started just below the belly button, carving a path that Jeffrey fully intended to follow.

"Let's see what you have hiding in here," Jeffrey said as he deftly opened the belt buckle and reached inside Ricardo's pants. "Hm. So soft. Does your God not make you happy?"

"Please," Ricardo croaked.

"You want me to help? Is that what you are asking?" Before he could answer, Jeffrey, reached a little deeper inside the pants, taking turns massaging Ricardo's scrotum and working the shaft. It was the equivalent of kneading dough, though, as the movements drew no response. Beginning to lose patience and control, Jeffrey hauled down the man's pants and underwear, taking the flaccid penis in his mouth and going at it with gusto. The response was the same, Ricardo's cock unwilling or unable to respond to the attention it was receiving.

Jeffrey could feel a red wave of rage washing over him, an uncontrollable surge of anger that threatened to crash against and destroy his last remaining vestiges of sanity. "COMPLIANCE," he roared, "How fucking difficult is it to do what I ask?"

Ricardo was sobbing then but was still unable to move.

"Open your mouth. Open that sweet fucking mouth of yours before I take off that useless little peg of yours."

Lips clenched tight, Ricardo shook his head, determined to fight despite the fact that he had very little left to give.

"What was that?" Jeffrey asked, responding to words unspoken. "Are you defying me? Well. If that is the case, then compliance and servitude must be taught. I'll ask you one more time; OPEN YOUR FUCKING MOUTH."

Before his head had barely made one trip from side to side, Jeffrey showed the point of the knife into Ricardo's scrotum, a twist of the blade eliciting a scream from the victim and a satisfying spray of blood on the hand holding the knife.

"You keep that mouth open, or things are about to get a whole lot worse for you, do you understand."

This time, Ricardo nodded, his jaws remaining spread wide as though held in place by a clamp.

Though already hard from his previous exertions, Jeffrey felt himself become fully engorged, the sight of blood and his victim finally playing along taking him to the next level. He gripped the young man's hair and pulled him closer to the edge of the table, dropping the knife and fumbling to free himself from the tight confines of his pants with his free hand.

"Open wide,' he said, forcing his swollen member into Ricardo's mouth, gagging him with the depth of the penetration.

Rocking his hips back and forth, Jeffrey eased into a rhythmic thrusting. Ricardo remained a little too slack-jawed, making it feel as though the cock was entering a cavern rather than a moist, tight mouth. Jeffrey pushed up on his victim's chin, closing the gap between top and bottom lips, creating a much stricter opening and a more sensual experience. With the feel of the lips on his shaft, his thrusting became more frantic and frenzied, the tightness in his balls making it clear that climax was fast approaching. When it arrived, Jeffrey exploded in Ricardo's mouth, the torrent of cum in the back of his throat once again triggering the gag reflex.

"Thank you for your compliance," Jeffrey said as he leaned over to kiss Ricardo, the taste of liquor replaced by the salty sex of his seed as their tongues touched. "Now, let's see if we can make you forever mine, shall we?"

Ricardo's eyes had glazed over, the young man having long since checked out from the reality of his situation. It was impossible to tell if he was in shock or simply still feeling the effects of the sedative. Either way, Jeffrey knew that the time was perfect for running the drill test. Past results had not been what he had hoped for, but the eternal optimist that lived inside his black heart told him that this was the one; this would be the test subject who passed with flying colors. With that in mind, he readied his tools and waited for a moment as another migraine sized shockwave hit him hard in the right temple.

Jeffrey snapped on a pair of surgical gloves, the latex scent blending with the aroma of fuck sweat and semen to create a heady miasma that most would have deemed an assault to the senses. To Jeffrey, it was the smell of creation. He tossed his head from side to side, inhaling in lungfuls of magnificent odor through his nostrils, feeling himself go hard once again. He knew he had to fight the urge, though, as there was work to be done before he could once again have his way with Ricardo. After all, they would have all the time in the world together once the test proved useful.

The drill bit was long and thin, the perfect size for the cranial insertion that it was about to be used for. Jeffrey dipped it into a beaker of diluted hydrochloric acid, making sure that the liquid coated every part of the bit. He gave it one more swirl for good measure before locking it into the electric drill that was charged and ready to work. After a few test spins, Jeffrey placed the drill bit against the young man's forehead and took one more deep breath before depressing the power button.

The drill jumped in his hand, the bit struggling to penetrate the thick bone that lay between the now ragged, torn open flesh. The electric hum of the drill turned into a high-powered whine akin to a dentist drill. Blood poured down Ricardo's face, streams of it pouring into his still open mouth. As the bit churned through the skull, a cloud of bone dust formed in the air in wispy, cumulus clouds shifting in the breeze created by Ricardo thrashing wildly on the table.

It was hard work, but before long Jeffrey began to sense that he was getting close to breaking through the skull entirely. He had performed this test often enough to become aware of the sounds that the drill bit made as it neared the end of its journey. Easing up on the power and the pressure a little, Jeffrey felt the bit reach its intended destination. The tricky part now was getting it out and moving on to the next task. The first time he had tried that, the bit had become fully wedged in the skull, only finally coming loose when the severed head had been soaked in the wasted barrel filled with acid. Flicking the drill into reverse, he slowly eased it up and out of the cranial channel, the bit coming clear with a satisfying sucking sound and another wave of blood.

Jeffrey waited for the flow of blood to decrease before wiping Ricardo's face and examining the hole that had been created. He was pleased to see that it was clean and that it might be his best effort yet. The belief that the experiment would work that time was beginning to grow with the outlook even better when he found a strong pulse and a steady heartbeat in his victim.

"I knew you were the one, Ricardo. What fun you are going to have serving me. Just one more and we will have the perfect family here. Are you ready to take the next step?"

Ricardo blinked slowly, a sign that Jeffrey took as a resounding yes.

Snapping off the soiled latex gloves, Jeffrey unhooked the top of the waste barrel in the corner, dropping them into the gruel contained within. As the gloves sank below the surface, bones and body parts rose to the top, breaching the surface like some malformed whale. The sight was captivating and caused Jeffrey's stomach to rumble with hunger. Refusing to be distracted by the fleshy smorgasbord, he put the lid back in place and snapped on a fresh pair of gloves.

"They say that cleanliness is next to Godliness, my sweet, so behold the care that I take to keep this process sanitized."

Jeffrey used a handful of disinfectant wipes to clean the area around the drill hole. The open space looked like the entrance to a tiny cave, the contents of which were waiting to be explored by some intrepid adventurer. Jeffrey had mined these routes in the past, but he had ultimately failed in his goal of creating a compliant being ready to serve his every sexual desire. It was those past failures that made him take his time with Ricardo.

Ditching the excess hydrochloric acid used to coat the drill bit, Jeffrey thoroughly cleaned the container, as well as the plastic funnel, which was brand new out of the packet. Convinced that both were as sterile as they could be in his current environment, he once again changed gloves and examined the hole in Ricardo's forehead. It looked like his best work yet, so he felt confident when he placed the end of the funnel into the hole, causing

Ricardo to grimace at what must have been an uncomfortable sensation.

Jeffrey could sense that his house guest was beginning to shake off the sedatives, so without wasting any more time, he carefully poured the contents of the container into the spout, watching in awe as the acid swirled around the funnel and made its way down into the cavity. Ricardo's body stiffened, his eyelids fluttering ever so slightly, as Jeffrey poured in the last of the acid, removed the funnel, and covered the hole with a band-aid. Throwing all the used pieces into the waste barrel, Jeffrey stepped back from the table, waiting to see if his experiment would deliver the desired results. He did not have to wait long.

Ricardo rolled over onto his side, emitting a low, guttural moan as a spray of vomit exploded from his mouth. The wave of nausea passed as quickly as it had arrived with Ricardo pushing himself up to a sitting position on the table.

"How do you feel?" Jeffrey asked.

"Different."

"Different, how?"

"Altered. More alive."

Before Jeffrey could say another work, Ricardo bolted off the table and launched an attack, a swinging right hand connecting squarely on Dahmer's jaw. Jeffrey's arms pinwheeled as he fell backward, the bed behind him breaking his fall, although the mattress suddenly felt hard and cold. Expecting a soft landing, Jeffrey was stunned when the back of his head connected with something substantial, causing the room to shift and tilt out of focus. He heard his name being yelled once more, but it was not Ricardo's voice. Instead, it seemed to come from off in the distance, drawing closer as the words being yelled echoed around the room.

The bedroom continued to spin on its axis as Jeffrey tried to get back to his feet. It was a futile task, as he simply felt too weak and disoriented. Laying back down, he took a more extended look around his bedroom, immediately seeing that things had changed rather dramatically. The space was cleaner than before, with the walls and ceiling drenched in a cold blue light being emitted from a trio of modern looking lamps suspended over his worktable. Spread evenly across the top were a collection of human skulls, with the black lacquered altar now flanked by a pair of skeletons.

"Beautiful," Jeffrey whispered.

No sooner were the words out of his mouth when he spotted movement in the corner of the room.

"Who's there?"

Ricardo stepped out of the gloom, his naked body seeming to shimmer once he entered the light cast by the overhead display. Staring at Jeffrey with a look of pure reverence, he said, "It is I, your humble servant, Ricardo. How may I serve you?"

Too stunned to speak, Jeffrey cast his gaze around the room, amazed that it was just as he had always dreamed. As his eyes adjusted to the light and his dizziness faded, he could see another figure standing in the corner across from Ricardo. The man, another magnificent creature, stepped forward, bowing ever so slightly as he entered into the light.

"We are here to serve," Ricardo and the other servant said in unison. "How shall we serve you, Master?"

Jeffrey choked back tears, the sight of such beauty in his presence, bringing up emotions that had laid long dormant. The rattling of the windowpane shook him from his reverie, the cold winter wind battering against his apartment. The distraction was abhorrent to Jeffrey, but his disdain quickly turned to delight as inspiration hit.

"Open the window. Let me hear them sing," he said.

Both servants bowed and moved in unison to the window, throwing it open in a style that made the simple act seem like a ceremonial ritual. The temperature in the room plummeted the moment Mother Nature's icy breath reached inside. The skeletons on the wall shook, the wind leading them in a grisly bone dance while the cold air whipped through the ocular cavities of the skeletons. The skulls appeared to howl, the wind passing through the open spaces creating a high-pitched whistle that brought goosebumps to Jeffrey's skin.

"Open your fucking eyes and look at me, Dahmer."

"My eyes are open."

"Open your eyes and look at me as you take your last fucking breath."

The voice was close now, close enough for Jeffrey to recognize. It was then that he opened his eyes and found himself on his back on the floor of a gymnasium. Blood pooled around him, warm, sticky, and flowing all too freely from the lacerations on his skull. It hurt to move, but Jeffrey tilted his head forward, just in time to see prison guards burst into the room and launch themselves at the man in the orange jumpsuit. He held a long metal bar, which was coated in blood, hair, and small white chunks that could have been teeth or bone fragments.

"Drop the weapon and hit the floor. Scarver," one of the guards hollered.

The man did as he was told, but he continued to yell, a piece of newspaper with Dahmer's face on it still clutched in his left hand. As the guards tackled Scarver to the floor, Jeffrey closed his eyes and tried to find his way back to his room and his beautiful servants, but all that he saw was darkness.

"Thanks for reading! If you enjoyed this book, I'd be very grateful if you'd post a short review. Your support really does make a difference, and I read all the reviews personally, so I can get your feedback and make my books even better.

Thanks again for your support!"

John Watson

Special Thanks

Thank you, as always, to the usual cast of characters who make it possible for me to continue creating stories. That includes my wife, Penny, Erin Lee and Crazy Ink, my PA, Diana Richie, and all of you who take the time to read what I put out. You are all greatly appreciated.

John Watson

Born under a gloomy, grey, Scottish sky, it is perhaps no real surprise that darkness has always felt comfortable to John Watson. After countless hours spent in his local library, he found that he was more at home in the worlds of Clive Barker, Stephen King, and James Herbert than he was in his own. The need to carve out his own niche in the horror genre drove Watson to slice open his mind and let the words spill onto the page.

From donuts to mysterious karaoke bars in the

middle of nowhere, Watson mines the depths of the ordinary to find the evil that lurks beneath the surface. He dares you to join him in his ongoing forays into the dark side.

John Watson's Novels and Novellas

Karaoke Night

Crueller

Off the Grid

Be Kind, Rewind

Cradle Robber

Slave to Blood

Swimming Upstream

Through the Eyes of the Mummy w/M.W. Brown

Anthologies

Infamy

Beyond the Jungle

Murder Maker

Follow John Watson

https://www.facebook.com/authorjohnwatson

Publisher's Note: This is a work of fiction. Names, characters, places, and incidents are a product of the author's imagination. Locales and public names are sometimes used for atmospheric purposes. Any resemblance to actual people, living or dead, or to businesses, companies, events, institutions, or locales is completely coincidental.

Made in the USA
Monee, IL
23 August 2021